Montana 4

Snow IN MONTANA

SNOW IN MONTANA

Snow In Montana, Montana 4
Copyright ©2016 RJ Scott
First Edition
Cover design by Meredith Russell
Edited by Sue Adams
Published by Love Lane Books Limited
ISBN 154-0-86-955-5

ALL RIGHTS RESERVED

DEDICATION

With thanks to my beta Elin for her firm assessment, to Sue for being awesome, and to my army of proofers, all of whom rock.

And always for my family.

FAMILY TREE

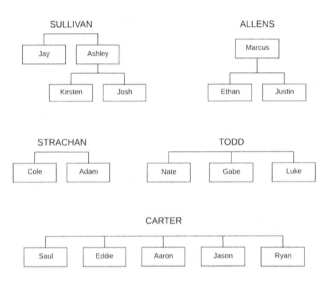

#1 - Crooked Tree Ranch – Nate & Jay's story
#2 - The Rancher's Son – Ethan & Adam's story
#3 - A Cowboy's Home – Justin & Sam's story
#4 - Snow in Montana – Ryan and Jordan's story

CHAPTER 1

~ *Ryan* ~

Ryan Carter watched the visitors arrive from the window of Marcus Allens' house. From his vantage point he could see two men and a woman get out of the rental car; one of the men had to be helped out, and the other two was fussing over him.

"Coffee?" Jay asked, passing a mug to Ryan.

"Thanks. Is that them?"

Ryan had been called into this meeting at Crooked Tree, to meet with representatives of Darby Films. Jay had said they needed advice on permits, but Ryan convinced himself it was just an excuse to have him sitting at the table in his uniform, lending a solid security presence to the discussions.

Jay was proud that Crooked Tree had been chosen as the location; the money they received for it would be responsible for helping Crooked Tree into the black this year. He'd promised the film company anonymity and security—Ryan's role in this.

"Yeah, that's them," Jay said. "Jordan and Micah Darby. They're twins and both used to be actors but Micah gave it up. The woman with them is their executive assistant, Angie Holmes."

"Don't know which it is," Ryan said and tapped the glass, "but one of the men looks drunk."

Jay let out a soft sigh. "LA types." He left to get his own coffee.

Ryan took a seat at the table, and when Jordan Darby finally walked in the room, Ryan was convinced his assessment was spot on. He prided himself on his ability to make quick judgments. In his job as sheriff, he was often put in situations that he had to size up immediately. He could look someone in the eyes and see their intentions, or at least be able to make an educated assumption.

All evidence pointed to Jordan Darby being hungover. Dark glasses hid his eyes, and he arrived at the meeting five minutes later than the other two.

Dark glasses. In February. Fuck's sake.

Five minutes in which Jordan's twin, Micah, and their PA, Angie, had to make small talk about the weather and the horses, and make excuses for the errant Jordan. Something about Jordan struggling with a cold.

Yeah, right.

Ryan didn't take long to make up his mind. Jordan was evidently a class-A douchebag who thought way too much of himself. His handshake was strong, but the mumbled hello that went with it had all the sincerity of an infomercial. When the man slumped into the nearest chair and looked pathetically at Angie, she fetched him coffee.

Yep. Douchebag.

The actor, production owner, whatever, fell on the coffee like it was lifeblood and hunched over it, wrapping both hands around the mug.

That's one hell of a hangover.

Jordan and Micah sat together, and Ryan noticed the differences straightaway. He'd read up on the Darby twins, on this Jordan, B-list actor and industry-acclaimed King of Christmas. His website was full of gushing reviews of movies with titles like *Twinkle at Christmas*, *The Holly Hook*, and several others, all with one thing in common: Christmas. Jordan had made a living from being the hero in made-for-TV romances, and he clearly had a high opinion of himself.

Micah leaned in and spoke to his brother quietly; Jordan side-eyed him and gave a subtle shake of his head.

Ryan watched the interaction and the small frown on Micah's face. He helped himself to more coffee before sitting, as unobtrusively as someone who came in at six-four could, at the opposite end of the table to the LA types. He hunkered down in the chair and sipped at the hot brew, looking over the rim of his cup at the rest of the people there. Every so often he would look back at Jordan, but the guy hadn't moved; he actually looked really pale and a little shaky, and Ryan's spidey senses went on alert. Was the man on something?

"Shall we start?" Jay asked.

Sam slipped into the seat next to Jay. Sam was in charge of catering for this venture while Jay project-managed the whole event. Jay didn't look fazed by the actor slumped in the chair, but then, that was Jay. Crooked Tree needed the business. Being used as a filming location was a feather in Jay's cap, and he was 200 percent behind making it work.

Whatever. He'd already roped Ryan in, citing security and permits, but Ryan was just here for the coffee and Ashley's amazing cakes. Any excuse to visit Crooked Tree was a good one.

Talking of which… he leaned over and helped himself to a blueberry and lemon muffin and a slice of apple sponge, then sat back, only to see Jordan had taken off his sunglasses and was blinking right at him. He had the most intense blue-gray eyes, and had Ryan been one to wax lyrical, he would call them the color of the storms that rolled in over the mountains and swept down the valleys.

They were also focused right on Ryan, then down at the plate before returning to him.

And then Jordan smiled at him. A perfect smile, with perfect white teeth. A smile that caused dimples to pop and made Ryan wonder what the hell Jordan was doing.

"Good cake?" Jordan asked. His voice was husky, and he finished on a cough into his hand.

Ryan arched a brow. "Very good." And then, as if he thought Jordan was going to walk over and steal what he'd chosen, he very deliberately took a bite of the muffin. Of course, that didn't go entirely according to plan, and he ended up with the sticky cake wedged to the roof of his mouth, which meant he couldn't say anything else. But still, these were *his* cakes.

"I want to apologize," Jordan said with that husky voice. He was talking to Jay alone now, his tone full of remorse. "I can't seem to shake this virus."

"Day four," Micah said, with an added huff and an elbow into Jordan's side.

"Can we get you anything?" Jay asked solicitously.

"A new set of lungs," Jordan said and then coughed again.

That actually made Ryan smile inwardly. For a douche, he was actually funny at that moment.

Jay chuckled and then handed around copies of the media pack that had come from Darby Films.

Ryan traced the logo with one finger. The logo was made to look like a heart, befitting a company that created romantic movies. After looking closer, he saw it was two pieces of film layered on top of each other in pink and orange. He skimmed the three-page letter; most of it talked about accommodation and catering, and only the penultimate paragraph dealt with security and regulations.

He'd already covered most of what he needed to do for his consultation fee, paid direct to the sheriff's department. It was tiring that his boss at County had such a hard-on for movies, because he'd said there was no way he was missing out on this kind of event in the ass end of Montana. Ryan thought he'd get away with phoning this in, but his friends Jay and Sam were here, waiting for his input.

"Nate has some specific requests regarding the use of ranch horses," Jay said, tapping the papers with the end of his pen.

Angie took that one. "We'll have on-site accreditation from the Humane Society. My notes say we have three scenes with the horses direct. Is that doable?"

"Absolutely," Jay said immediately. "Nate is the man you need to talk to when you begin filming."

Angie noted that. "Nate Todd, am I right? I've already spoken to him directly. Will we be meeting him today?"

Jay looked pained but quickly covered it up.

Ryan had seen that look before and had witnessed Nate being all stubborn about not coming down from his work with the horses just to schmooze with city types. Ryan was totally behind that train of thought... and yet here he was anyway.

"He's out on a trail," Jay said.

"I thought the ranch was closed to guests?" Angie asked, with concern lacing her tone. "We were told we had full run of the space."

"No guests," Jay said, clearly realizing he'd dug a hole trying to explain away Nate's absence. "Just horse work."

Ryan bit his lip. That was lame. He glanced over at Jordan and saw the man staring right at him. Again. Ryan deliberately looked away and focused back on Jay, who changed the subject. He listened to Jay summarize what they had so far, and then they reached the part Ryan could talk about and he straightened a little.

"The sheriff's brother is with the fire department," Jay began, turning the conversation right over to Ryan, who was wishing right about then that he'd managed to get out of this meeting like Nate had.

Ryan was the youngest of five brothers. Jason, the next youngest, was a fireman; the middle sibling a paramedic; next up an accountant; and his oldest brother, Saul, owned a local bar. Ryan was nothing if not prepared for all eventualities, and he had a sense of pride when he talked about them; all their own men despite their shitty start in life.

He began, "I asked Jason about the regulations for pyrotechnics, and he's escalated it to Division."

"Does the division foresee any circumstances where we would need to cut down on the scenes we require?" Angie asked.

"Well, I saw Jason at dinner last night and he said he was happy with everything—" Ryan began.

"That's not what I asked," Angie said, in an efficient, icy tone. "This firefighter, Jason, may be your brother, but we need an expert's opinion in writing. Not your say so that someone is happy with what he's seen."

Ryan didn't like her tone and he went from relaxed to formal in an instant. If official was what she wanted then that was what she was going to get. "Lieutenant Jason Carter has run the assessments, and signed off on the location, and has confirmed in writing, that he has escalated any issues that he felt needed addressing."

Angie winced. "Sorry, I meant no offense."

Micah interjected. "This is Darby Films' first location shoot, I think we're all a little bit on edge and want everything to go well."

Shit. Now Ryan felt guilty. He'd definitely come over as territorial and defensive. Added to which, Jay was now looking at him pointedly, which made him feel worse.

And Jordan was still looking at him too, which made him think he had crumbs on his chin, or his hair was sticking up or something. He wasn't the kind of guy who stood for hours in front of a mirror fussing over his hair, which stubbornly curled around his face. His hair was just a little too long, parted at one side, and fell in two heavy bangs—not quite sheriff-style, but he always attempted to keep it regulation length.

Well, most of the time.

He very likely *did* have crumbs all over him. Cake was his thing; he had a weakness for them, but his tall frame could carry it off and his belly wasn't overly soft.

Yet.

According to his brothers, Ryan was the most likely to end up looking like a teddy bear, all cuddly. Self-consciously he wiped his face with a napkin and glanced down at the front of his uniform to check for crumbs. Then he rested one hand on his belly, which was mostly tight and flat, *thank you very much, asshole brothers.*

"Can we talk catering?" Angie said, and Ryan settled into listening, or at least pretending to listen.

Sam launched into a summary of what he would be doing with Ashley, all enthusiasm and big grins. Sam made Ryan nervous in ways he didn't want to have to think about. The man flirted unashamedly, or he had until he'd hooked up with Justin.

That was who Sam was, and for some time Ryan had a thing for him. Who wouldn't? Sam was this bundle of focused energy, cute, sexy, and funny. He was also very much off the market now, in love with Justin, and Ryan had left it just that little bit too late to approach Sam for a date. Not that he ever stood a chance with Sam anyway. Because, to get a date, you'd at least need to talk to the man you wanted to ask out.

Jordan coughed again and Angie went to get more coffee, which Jordan took with a grateful smile. Ryan watched her press a hand to Jordan's forehead and grimace, but Jordan didn't move away.

Clearly the sexy, stormy-eyed, B-list actor who stared at Ryan was taken.

"Let's talk finance," Micah said from Jordan's side. Jordan relaxed abruptly as Micah took over. "We've paid the deposit and permit payments. When we talked, you were happy with the structured payments, with the bulk to be paid after March 27. We appreciate this isn't how things normally work, but we are a new company, and as such we'd like to release our investment in stages."

"We can work with that."

"We don't want you in the red in any way, though," Micah added. "And every payment will be made before we leave site."

"When do you think that will be?" Ryan asked, because he felt like he should be saying something.

"March 31," Angie said. "The filming is scheduled up until March 23, but we'd like some leeway, so the booking is from this weekend until the end of March."

"Six weeks," Jordan added and coughed again.

Ryan winced. Half at the rasping sound, half because of the germs now circulating the room. Not that he was ever ill, but still, it wasn't professional of this actor be here and be coughing over everyone, right?

Micah laid a hand on Jordan's arm and squeezed it, and Jordan nodded. "I need to get some air," he announced. "I'll leave the rest to Micah and Angie."

He shook hands with Jay, then Sam, and finally Ryan. "Could I talk to you outside?" he asked Ryan as he released his hold.

Ryan glanced at Jay, who shrugged. Obviously, he didn't know what was up.

"Sure." Ryan refilled his coffee mug and followed Jordan outside.

Today was particularly bright, the sun startling against the crystals of snow, and Ryan wished he hadn't left his sunglasses in the car. Jordan winced at the light and slipped on his own glasses before leading him down to the bridge and the shade of the huge trees by the water. The air was frosty, but they both had thick jackets. Only Jordan was shivering. LA Boy probably wasn't used to a Montana winter.

"You need a better coat," Ryan informed him, then bit his lip because this was a client for Crooked Tree and he'd already fucked up with defending his brother.

"I know." Jordan wrapped his hands around himself, hopping rather pathetically from foot to foot. "Not much call for thick winter coats in LA," he added. Then he glanced up at the sky.

Ryan wished he could see the stormy eyes, get a closer look at them to see whether they were bluer out here, less steel gray.

"I bet," Ryan offered lamely. There was something about Jordan that had him feeling off-balance. That air of vulnerability from being sick, with the shine of money and designer clothes, the beauty of a perfect face with gorgeous eyes, and the whole staring thing.

"So, I have this security thing...." Jordan shivered again.

Ryan took his arm and led him down to his cruiser, opened the door and gestured inside, then climbed into the driver's side and turned on the heater. Jordan seemed grateful, opening his coat after a while and resting his head back on the headrest.

"What kind of a security thing? That sounds pretty vague. I have protocols, but unless you think people knowing you're here will cause a stampede of fans to invade us, I doubt we'll have much to worry about."

Jordan smiled then, a soft smile, and he pressed his fingers to his temples. "No, I don't have those kind of fans, and we're in the middle of nowhere."

Ryan wasn't going to take exception to that. Crooked Tree might be part of the center of his universe, but that didn't mean Jordan wasn't right about it being kind of isolated out here.

"I had an issue last year," Jordan continued. He picked at the hem of his jersey. "Shit, this is embarrassing."

"We're covered by cop-client confidentiality," Ryan announced.

"That's a thing?" Jordan sounded surprised.

"Not really, but what's said in the car stays in the car."

"Last year I filmed this Cinderella story, a movie version, of course, based loosely on the darker concepts of the original Cinderella, not the fluffy and cute Disney version. Thing is, this guy in the local town, he took exception to the story and to me—hell, he took exception to everything—and he came at me with a car." Jordan frowned. "Not a good time."

"Arrested?"

"Damn right. My management took it very seriously. The guy is in jail, receiving psychiatric care. He had this whole photo wall of actors. Not just me—this isn't a cliché of a stalker and an actor, I promise you. Just, I wanted to let you know this has happened to me. Before, I mean."

"Okay, I'll make a note."

"And—" Jordan sighed noisily. "—there's something else that might be a bit more worrying."

"Which is?"

"There's this journalist, Thomas Ivory, who wants the 'scoop' on my family."

Jordan used his fingers to air quote around scoop. He didn't need to; Ryan could already hear the distaste in his voice.

"Your family. Not just you, but your brother as well?"

"And my mom. But she's with husband number four and he's rich as hell, so no hack is getting anywhere near her. It's more that my dad died young, not long after we were born, actually. You should google him." He sank back against the seat, exhaustion bracketing his eyes.

"You're saying this journalist might turn up here?"

"Maybe. I have a restraining order, I can get you a copy."

Ryan hadn't come across a celebrity-stalker situation before in his work, but he'd seen a lot of things very close. He wasn't going to reassure Jordan with blanket statements that he would look after him—that wasn't him. He had to be firm and honest. "That would be useful. Also, anything like that happens here, you can report to me and I will make sure the proper authorities are involved."

Jordan seemed relieved, tension slipping from him until he looked boneless in the seat. At least he'd stopped coughing.

"Have you seen a doctor?" Ryan asked after a moment's silence.

"Hmm." Jordan shut his eyes. "I'm on antibiotics," he added in a whisper.

And then, between one heartbeat and the next, he was asleep.

Right there in Ryan's vehicle, his mouth slightly open, his face flushed with heat and his breathing slightly labored, Jordan the B-lister was asleep. His sunglasses had tilted a little, and Ryan carefully removed them, at the same time wondering how the hell he was going to explain this if Jordan woke up.

Jordan didn't. He murmured something and slumped lower in the seat.

Ryan sat there for a moment. What did you do when a guy fell asleep in your car?

And then it hit him. He'd get Angie, and she could deal with him

He left the car and went back to Jay's office. As he let himself in, everyone looked at him.

"Hey," he said to Angie. "Your boyfriend is asleep in my car."

Angie looked surprised and glanced at Micah, who shook his head in some silent conversation.

"Is he okay?" Micah asked.

"Ill," Ryan said, like he even had to mention that. "He's in my car. Asleep."

Micah grimaced. "Sheriff, can we please leave him for a while? He's not slept well in days now. Unless it's too cold. We should move him, right?"

Micah looked so damn earnest, and his gray eyes, not as dark as Jordan's, held concern. Ryan bristled at the manipulation, but at the end of the day, Jordan sleeping in his car wasn't that much of an inconvenience and was a reason to stay longer at Crooked Tree.

"I wrapped a space blanket over him, but you'll need to check on him, okay?"

"I'll go," Angie announced, and bundled into a coat to leave.

Ryan helped himself to more coffee, because hell, he was already buzzing with it, so why not add to the effect. Then he took another muffin, vowing to go for a run as soon as he got home.

And he didn't think about the man in his car, or his gorgeous eyes, or the fact that the man was a client of Crooked Tree Ranch.

He just ate muffins, drank coffee, and contemplated his run.

CHAPTER 2

~ *Jordan* ~

"I'm sorry, Micah," Jordan said for the thirtieth time that day. He couldn't help himself; he had the energy of a limp noodle, and his brother had taken on most of the work that Jordan would normally do.

"Stop saying that and get back into bed."

Jordan hovered in the doorway. He had things to do; this company was him *and* Micah, not something Micah should be carrying on his own. This flu had knocked Jordan to the ground, but he wasn't surprised; the last year had been hard, manic, awful... no wonder he was ill.

"I'm bored in bed." And yes, he was aware he was whining, but he'd had enough, and the hotel bed was like rock, hard and unyielding. Tomorrow they were moving to Crooked Tree, and he hoped to hell the beds were bigger and softer and he could get decent sleep.

"There's nothing for you to do."

"What about Debbie? Is she flying out today or tomorrow?"

Debbie Stevens, female lead, was another of the actors who'd made their careers in made-for-TV movies. She was to act opposite him in this classic Christmas romance of the down-on-her-luck single mom to his small-town cop, on a ranch in the snow, with horses, a couple of kittens, maybe a puppy, all set in Montana. The script actually made sense, but when it was summarized like that, it sounded so cliché.

Who was he kidding, everything he did was cliché; he wasn't called the King of Christmas for nothing. Jordan had done eight of these Christmas movies now, and he was damn good at them. He privately loved romance with all its familiar storylines.

Micah sighed his best put-upon sigh. "Debbie is already in Missoula. The driver is picking her up from the hotel at 0700 for script read-through. As are Jim, Stefanie, and the new intern, Shawna, not to mention the rest of the crew who're a couple of hours out. So, we're set."

"What about the girl playing the daughter?" He couldn't remember her name, his head full of scrambled thoughts.

"Emma, her name is Emma, and she is coming in with her mom tomorrow, her tutor the day after."

"And the—"

"Jordan, seriously. Get some sleep. I'll come find you if I need you."

"Micah—"

Micah huffed, which stopped Jordan talking, then stood and they had a face-off. It would have been comical had Jordan not felt like shit. "Look, little brother," Micah began in that brotherly way he had of getting under Jordan's skin.

They were born twenty-two minutes apart, so Micah was only a little older, but it was his go-to insult. He hadn't finished.

"I'm in charge out here. You're the actor, and I'm the one who makes the acting happen. Now go to bed."

"Did you see anything from Ivory? Has he updated his blog?"

"I checked. There's nothing more on there about Dad."

"What if he tracks us down, it's not a secret where we're filming?"

"Go to bed."

"Micah, I'm being serious—"

"So am I. No one will find out about you, or make up shit about Dad, least of all a talentless hack like Ivory."

For a second, Jordan was being swayed, but the familiar fear still held him. Living with fear seemed to be his permanent problem. "Are we doing the right thing?" he asked, defeat edging his voice.

Micah's stern expression shifted a little, and for a moment it showed vulnerability. "Yes."

"All of our money, though. What if we fuck this up? What if the movie is shit because I fuck up?"

Something about what he said or possibly how pathetic he looked made Micah pull him in for a close hug. "You won't fuck this up, I won't fuck this up. Please, go back to bed because otherwise I'll call 911 and tell them you collapsed. And by the way, you're gross. You need a freaking shower."

"Fuck you," Jordan managed, the effect ruined when his chest tightened and he was headed for another coughing fit.

He made it back to his room and into the bathroom before the coughing began. Drinking water helped; getting into the shower and washing away a night of restless sleep helped further. Then he settled into the other bed in his room, where the sheets were clean and cool. He pulled open his laptop. A few keystrokes and he had called up his go-to work in progress, the kind of film he'd love to make.

Where a man fell in love with a man, in a real gay romance, and the movie was shown to mainstream audiences, and there was no hate, only acceptance.

Micah teased him, but his twin had his back for them to make the film in their five year plan. They'd probably generate no income from it; maybe they'd need to crowdfund.

Of course, if he was going to be in a gay movie, he'd probably have to admit to the world at large that Jordan Darby, confirmed heterosexual lead for eight separate romances, was, in fact, gay.

He worked on the manuscript for a while, hesitating at the edits in the lead-up to the sex scene. He'd already scripted an angry kiss—in the rain, of course. But the connection between the two leads he had in his head wasn't there. He wasn't feeling the love.

Was that because he hadn't experienced love?

Lust? Well, he'd had a bucketful of that. Careful, controlled lust in private with guys who had reasons to keep their mouths shut. Not real lust, then, because lust wasn't something you controlled; lust was fire and need and life.

What he'd had was getting off. Simple as that. Twenty-nine, turning thirty in a month, and he had never connected romantically with anyone.

As a headache began to form behind his eyes, Jordan closed his laptop, lay down, and snuggled under the covers.

Too hot.

He removed the covers.

Too cold.

With a muttered curse, he pulled the covers up to his neck, then pushed one leg out from under them.

Better.

He needed to sleep. The last decent sleep he'd had was yesterday in Sheriff Carter's car.

Shame heated his face. He couldn't believe he'd done that, fallen asleep, probably snoring and drooling all over Sexy Cop's car. He'd just been so tired, exhausted even, and then the flu had hit him and turned into something worse, and he couldn't stay awake. But Ryan hadn't complained; he'd left him in the car, and it had been Micah who had woken him up and led him to the rental car they'd hired to take him back to the hotel.

Jordan didn't see Ryan before he left, and that was a shame. He might not see him again, apart from a couple of review visits, and there was something about the sheriff that meant Jordan could *not* look away.

He was big—six four or five—and his hair had this floppy, don't-care kind of appeal. His dark gaze had kept flicking to Jordan as a small frown creased his forehead. Jordan liked to think, with his drug-addled, sleepy brain, that Ryan had been checking him out. And for a few moments, he actually contemplated doing something about it by working out which team big Sheriff Sexy played for. Because he was everything Jordan liked, not to mention the man also loved cakes. Which meant under that uniform, despite the muscles, there may be a softness to him. In Jordan's mind, there was nothing better than lying in bed, head on a soft belly, feeling the strength under there. Particularly when his lover could pick him up, maybe lift him and arrange him just so, before fucking him into tomorrow.

There was also Ryan's hands. Jordan hadn't been able to stop looking at them: big, strong, and capable, and the muffin had looked so tiny as he held it.

All that on top of pills for his chest infection and lack of sleep, which made him tired and loopy.

Finally, when his cock actually made a valiant effort to rise at the thought of Ryan holding him still, he cursed at life and turned onto his front. He nestled into the pillow, moved his leg out from where it had tangled as he turned, then closed his eyes.

He was not fucking about on his doorstep. Especially not after nearly being hit by a car after the Cinderella movie and having a journalist waiting for him to make a mistake.

Jordan had a company to build, a commitment to his brother, to Angie, and to the staff they had back at the office; the whole team that supported this new venture.

He just couldn't afford to be openly out there, not right now.

With that decision made, and ignoring the warning tightness in his head, he slept.

When Jordan arrived at Crooked Tree, he landed slap-bang in the middle of chaos.

Despite his nagging headache, the chaos made him smile.

This was bedlam he understood: trucks unloading equipment, people buzzing around with clipboards and notepads, others huddled in groups, some talking into radios.

"Jordan!" He turned at Angie's voice. "Jay gave us his office. Come on."

Jordan followed Angie from the parking lot over the bridge and up to Jay's office. It seemed like a lifetime since the meeting followed by the embarrassment of falling asleep in the car, but it had been less than forty-eight hours. At least he felt marginally better; the knot of pain in his chest had eased a little and his head felt clearer. He was still ill, but by the time they started filming in a few days, he'd be awake enough to pass for human.

"Do I need to move some scenes around on the schedule?" Angie asked, leaning on the side of the desk.

"Just give me a couple more days."

"On it. Oh, and Debbie arrived. We've put her in the first cabin. She brought her kids with her, but no sign of the husband. Word is that things have gone south there." She indicated her clipboard. "Micah is down at the cabins with the allocations. You're with Micah and me, okay?"

Jordan half smiled. He could stand to be around his brother, but he had something to add to the arrangement.

"We could actually fit another crew member in our cabin," Jordan said and turned to look at the stunning photographs on the wall. Some of them he recognized from the Crooked Tree website, the same site that spoke of stunning views, the Blackfoot River, and a hundred other things that made this place perfect.

"No, we can't. There's only three rooms." Angie sounded confused. "Me, you, and Micah. Three people, three rooms."

Without turning, Jordan shrugged. "Angie, you and I both know that as soon as he thinks I am asleep that he'll be heading into your room for the night. No sense in wasting a room."

He heard the sharp inhalation of breath and turned to face her. He was happy for Micah, and he loved Angie. She'd been his PA since the moment he got his first contract with Hallmark. And she and Micah were meant for each other.

"I...." She stopped, evidently lost for words.

"Just give in already. You're good together, and I think it's wonderful."

"You do?"

She looked surprised. Why was she startled? "Of course, I do. You're so happy together."

"Just..."

"Just what?"

"Jordan, you and Micah been taking this new company so seriously, and you have so much pressure, both of you, that we thought... it hasn't been long."

"I know. It was the wrap party for the last Hallmark film, right? *Autumn Fall*?"

"Did Micah tell you?"

"Nope, I have eyes. Come here." He held out his hands and stepped closer, and she walked into a hug. They hugged often. Jordan was tactile, loved to hug. "Do me a favor and go public."

"I don't want anyone to think I am the executive assistant because I'm sleeping with one of the bosses," she admitted against his chest.

"We're not your bosses, you own part of Darby Films, and hell, everyone loves you."

She hesitated and worried her lower lip with her teeth. "It doesn't seem fair though."

"In what way?" Although he had the feeling he knew exactly what was going on behind her eyes. She was doing that whole *worrying about Jordan* thing.

"You don't get to have a boyfriend on set."

And there it was.

He sighed. "Angie, that's not an issue you need to worry about. I might need to have secrets, but you don't."

At that, Angie gripped him hard. She knew what he had to hide and why he did it, and she said the same thing every time.

"You could come out, then go behind the camera if people don't like it. You'd still have us."

Jordan considered that he and Micah had sunk every penny of their inheritance into Darby Films, and he smiled to himself. He would be happy in the shadows a little while longer, being able to act, and having hook ups on the side. This company was important to him, and his five year plan was in place and starting already. When Darby Films was finally riding the high of success, he could reveal bits of himself a little at a time, and everything would be okay. No one would run articles about the irony of a gay man playing straight leads, or any of the other shit he could imagine happening.

The door opened and Micah walked in, stomping his boots free of snow, his breathing labored.

There was complete silence.

Micah looked from Angie to Jordan and back again. "What happened?"

Angie eased herself from Jordan's hold and crossed straight to him, cradling his face, holding him tight, and kissing him deeply.

All Jordan could do was chuckle at his brother's startled stare over the kiss. *One secret down.*

Then she left.

"Jordan—"

"The wrap party for *Autumn Fall*, two beers back at her room. Yes, she's perfect for you, and yes, I'm very happy for you."

Micah's face fell and he crossed his arms over his chest. "Okay, so you know. Is that okay?"

"I love Angie. Like I said, she's perfect for you," Jordan reassured. "Hurry up and make me an uncle. Just remind her, in case it isn't obvious, that twins run in our family."

Micah blanched. "I got a ring," he whispered, as if Angie was in the room and could hear him.

So, then it was Jordan's turn to pull Micah in for a hug. They didn't need words; the hug was everything. It was 'I love you, brother' and 'I'm happy for you' all wrapped in one embrace.

"Back at it, then," Micah said, and they parted with some manly backslaps. "We have to consider snow."

"What about snow?"

"Backup in case it all melts."

"We have snow. Lots of snow. We chose here *because* of the snow," Jordan said.

"Contingency in case it melts."

"Shit? Will it melt overnight?"

"I don't know."

"If it does, then I want real snow, not that fake shit that gave me a reaction last year." He leaned back on the desk, suddenly tired.

"It wasn't the snow you had a reaction to; it was the amount of coffee you were drinking."

"I was playing a character with a rod up his ass," Jordan defended. "I was bored with acting a boring character, and I needed coffee."

Angie stepped back in. Snow swirled in with her, and Jordan looked at Micah, with a nod to the white stuff.

"Okay, no snow machine," Micah conceded.

"I need to talk tax breaks," Angie said.

"I need a good cup of coffee," Micah said.

Jordan scrubbed his eyes. Setting up Darby Films was a step into the great unknown, and if he'd known how much he'd have to consider, then maybe he would have thought twice about starting this up. Yes, he had Micah on one side and Angie on the other, but he was an actor—what did he know about location scouting or permits or tax breaks? For a moment, it all felt like too much.

"Tax breaks?" he asked her weakly, tired and lacking caffeine. "Statewide for filming? I thought we'd gone through that."

"We have some hoops to jump through. I need signatures from both of you."

Micah signed immediately and passed it back, and to be honest, so did Jordan. Angie had a stake in the success of Darby Films as much as they did, even if it was for a smaller amount of principal invested, it was as important to her. Particularly if she was going to be marrying Micah soon.

"I have a couple of things on my list," she said.

"What?" He couldn't help the worried tone or the instant anxiety. Sue him—he was still ill.

"We need to sign off on more public liability courtesy of our friendly sheriff, and also one of the cabins has no heating, but Jay is on that and we'll be up and running by tomorrow. Meanwhile we're doubling up."

He recalled the day they chose Crooked Tree over another place, one that had way more accommodation than they needed.

They'd looked at both on the laptop. The other ranch, on the Big Sky Blue website, was indeed mostly blue. Lots of freaking shades of the color—water, sky, accommodation painted in sapphire-and-gray stripes. The only thing that wasn't blue was the grass. Still, Big Sky Blue had been sprawling, with promised quiet corners, stunning views, and real-life cowboys.

Jordan had always had a thing for cowboys. And cops. And doctors. As long as they were big and handsy, he could go for any of them.

There'd been the usual pictures of horses, saddles, fields, the sapphire ranch house. And he could have worked with the color. Maybe they could have renamed the movie, called it *Blue Christmas* or something, although that would have inferred the plot was miserable.

Then there had been Crooked Tree with its less colorful website, relying instead on a simple gallery of photos with few words and dropdowns for all kinds of things. There was a restaurant there, Branches, that had some good write-ups, and so many cowboys, and horses, and trail rides. Still, from the photos it looked less accessible than the other one, more in a valley than flat land, but it did have a bridge over the water, which fitted the fight scene in the second act.

Crooked Tree was rugged and extended up onto the mountain; Big Sky was flat, backing toward the mountains. One had the river, the other, rolling pastures. They discovered there had been some drama at Crooked Tree a while back, which Micah pointed out might be good for marketing.

But when it had come to the bottom line, Angie was honest. "Crooked Tree is cheaper."

He just hoped that going for cheaper didn't mean problems. Cheaper was better on paper, but this was the first movie they were doing on their own, without Hallmark behind them, and without network support. He didn't want to live to regret it.

"You won't know if you don't try," Mom had told him, with her usual wisdom.

Of course, it wasn't Mom laying everything on the line here.

Nope, it was just him, Micah, and their five-year plan.

Year one: make a movie and sell it for a television audience, make a small profit or at least break even. Years two and three: much the same, but with three movies in the year and a bigger profit. Year four was three movies again, but with one of them focusing on a gay couple. And year five? That was to be the year that Jordan Darby came out of the closet, with a solid company behind him, and made a movie where he could be one of the gay leads, and it would sell, and he would leave a mark on this world he could be proud of.

Just a modest target, then.

CHAPTER 3

~ *Ryan* ~

"Morning, Sunshine," Saul said and slid a coffee across the table.

Ryan took it and grunted his thanks. His brother knew there was no way he would be capable of much rational speech this early in the morning, and they'd dropped into this system whereby perpetually cheerful Saul, the oldest of five boys, made everything better. How Saul could be this awake at 5:00 a.m., Ryan didn't know.

Saul ran a bar. Carter's Bar was his baby, and even though he had staff, he couldn't have closed much before 2:00 a.m.

"What time do you need to be at Crooked Tree?"

Ryan glanced at his watch, but it was a blurry mess without his glasses or contacts. "Six."

Something bumped his hand and he glanced sideways at the plate of toast.

"Eat," Saul ordered.

"Yes, Dad," Ryan snarked, then took a few bites. It was coffee he really wanted, and Sam might well have food he could scrounge when he got to the ranch. Or maybe Ashley had baked. Still, the toast helped, and the coffee began to work to sharpen his senses.

"Eddie is bringing the kids up on the weekend," Saul said.

Ryan didn't have to look to know that Saul had his ever-present diary notebook out on the table. Somehow the eldest Carter hadn't let go of that need to look after all his brothers. There were columns for all of them in age order, and in there, Ryan knew, there would be notes of his shifts and anything else Ryan had mentioned. Saul was eighteen years and three days older than Ryan, and the other three Carter boys ranged in the middle.

Saul had been just old enough to take responsibility for his brothers at eighteen, including the baby Ryan. "How is he?"

"You'd know if you called him," Saul admonished in that soft tone that made Ryan feel guilty in an instant.

"Last time I called he hung up on me," he explained.

Saul muttered something and then sighed. "Saying you were going to do a background check on his new girlfriend will do that to a guy."

"After what Sarah did to him—"

"It's not our business, and Jenny is lovely, and she's good with the kids."

"Says the brother who knows exactly where we are and what we're doing every minute of every freaking day."

Saul changed the subject. "Thought we'd do a barbecue. Be here at noon?"

Ryan wanted to point out he wasn't going to be anywhere else. He was on duty until eleven. He lived over the bar, sharing the apartment with Saul, so of course he'd be here.

"I'll be there."

Saul scratched something in the diary—probably some kind of tick in the attendance column.

"Bring a friend," Saul said, his tone that infuriating mix of hope and interference. "How about Mark? I liked him. He was nice."

Ryan was really not going *there* at 5:00 a.m. in the freaking morning. Mark had lasted exactly a week, right to the point when Mark explained how he wanted him and Ryan to have an open relationship.

"Back off," he snarled, snapped, and laced it with a little brother's patented whine. Then he pushed his chair back and stomped out of the kitchen.

"Ryan and Mark, sitting in a tree," Saul shouted after him.

"Whatever." He grimaced as he took the steps up to his room two at a time. At least now he was awake.

A shower, his contacts, and dressed in uniform, and he was back in the kitchen. One last coffee and he was out to his car.

When he arrived at Crooked Tree, he walked into chaos. Or at least it looked like chaos to him, but to everyone walking in and out of trailers in the parking lot it was probably highly organized chaos.

"Ryan!"

He turned to face the owner of the voice, spotted Sam and Justin just inside a large tent, and decided that direction was as good as any. He wanted to check in with Justin, see how the man was doing. A couple of people nodded at him, muttered "Officer" or "Sheriff," but no one stopped to talk. Everyone had something to do, and Ryan wound his way past wires and boxes to what he assumed was the catering tent.

Justin had gone before he got there, leaving Sam and a table groaning with food. Two young guys there, both in chef's whites, were clearly assisting with the burden of catering for however many people were present.

"Twenty-seven," Sam explained, "but I catered for more, so help yourself."

Ryan didn't hesitate; he grabbed a plate of eggs, crispy bacon, and fluffy pancakes, and stood back in the corner, checking his watch every so often. Ten minutes to go and he'd cleared his plate while watching Sam doing his thing, ordering around his two assistants.

Still no sign of Justin coming back.

In fact, Justin did a very good job of avoiding Ryan, and with ten minutes to kill, Ryan decided to zip up his coat and go looking. Something about the way Justin wouldn't quite look him in the eye had him feeling off. Justin had secrets—he'd been working for some shadowy kill squad after vanishing years ago with Adam. There was no information that Ryan could dig up, a blank of years that frustrated his analytical law enforcer's brain.

He finally found his quarry standing with Marcus, hands in his pockets and a stony expression on his face. Marcus had been overwhelmed getting his son back, and Justin had tried hard to fit back into Crooked Tree life, but it was plain to see there was tension between father and son. When Ryan observed the two of them together, he often thought the pressure was going to snap into something more, but there was always a rigidity about Justin. The guy only truly relaxed when he was with Sam.

Justin saw him coming, lifted his chin, and stared. "Sheriff," he said, with a nod.

"Ryan," he emphasized, and not for the first time. "Call me Ryan."

They were surely friends more than professional acquaintances. Being five years older than Justin meant they'd never been at school together, but still... more than just acquaintances, surely.

Another nod and Justin pressed his lips into a thin line. Ryan just knew that Justin wouldn't be calling him by his first name.

Then they ran out of things to say. Or rather, Ryan wanted to ask questions and Justin didn't want to answer them. They'd fallen into this weird, stony face-off, and Marcus had long since left.

"Can I talk to you?" Justin asked.

Ryan frowned and looked left and right. Justin was actually addressing him, right? "Of course."

"Not here, not now. I'll text you."

And then he slipped away, sidestepping Ryan in one of his freaky ninja moves, and by the time Ryan made it to the front of the tent, Justin had vanished again.

Well, that wasn't at all covert and weird. He shook his head and stepped out into the icy early morning half-light.

"Hey," someone said from his side, "Good morning, Sheriff."

Jordan was there, in so many layers of coats and scarves that it was difficult to see any more than a thin strip of his face, but Ryan would recognize those eyes anywhere. Then he remembered Jordan had a twin; was this Micah? They hadn't looked the mirror image of each other, and Ryan couldn't recall the color of Micah's eyes.

Which reminded him he needed to google the man and find out about the father, then look for photos of Jordan and his twin, Micah.

For information purposes only, obviously.

"Hey," Ryan said, abruptly very unsure.

Something in his tone must have shown hesitation because Jordan—or possibly Micah—pushed down the scarves from his face.

"Jordan. Remember me? I fell asleep in your car."

Ryan held out a hand and they shook, which wasn't easy when both were wearing heavy gloves.

Jordan kept talking, his voice less gruff than it had been two days ago, and he was staring right at Ryan.

For a second, Ryan imagined he had egg on his face and dismissed the idea. Just because a guy stared at him didn't mean he had food on his face. He hadn't the last time, and he didn't now.

Still, he brushed at his mouth with his gloved hand, just in case, because Jordan made him feel like he wanted to look perfect.

What the hell? Where did that come from?

"I'm sorry about that, by the way," Jordan carried on. "I usually don't go sleeping in sheriffs' cars." He smiled, and Ryan's brain short-circuited because, fuck, dimples.

"You spend a lot of time in sheriffs' cars?" Ryan asked before his brain caught up with his mouth. *I'm losing it.*

Jordan shook his head. "No, I guess not. I was dosed up and ill."

"I know." And then he recalled the usual thing that normal people might say at this point. Normal, sane, rational, people. "Are you feeling better?"

Jordan wrapped his hands around himself and stamped a bit. "Much. Just freaking cold."

Ryan searched his brain for an answer to that one while trying not to lose himself staring into those gray eyes. "It's Montana," he said lamely.

Jordan chuckled, coughed a little. "So it is. You want me to show you around?"

Ryan didn't want to take Jordan away from whatever he was supposed to be doing, so he said, "I can do my own thing."

"No, it's okay. Follow me."

Jordan pivoted and led Ryan through the maze of tents and wires, stopping and explaining that this was Production, this was their version of a green room, and this was Editing.

Ryan spoke to everyone, got a feel for the way things were running, and filed away as much information as he could. There wasn't much he could say, although he had a list of things he needed to check when they were somewhere warmer. Not for his sake—he was plenty warm enough, a Montana native with enough layers to make him look like a snowman—but Jordan still hadn't got the idea and he was shivering under the coat. Which had Ryan considering one question they hadn't covered…

"How will you film outside scenes without coats?"

Jordan looked a little panicked for a moment, but it soon cleared and cheerful optimism seemed to carry him through. "We'll be fine."

Ryan didn't want to point out that this was early in the day, and if there were night shoots, Jordan was in danger of becoming a Popsicle.

Jason arrived a little after nine, in uniform and clearly just off shift judging by the tiredness bracketing his eyes.

"Hey, little brother," he said on a yawn.

That was the way he always addressed Ryan, but somehow, in front of Jordan, Ryan didn't want to be identified as little. Then, Jason held out a hand, and he and Jordan did that whole awkward glove-slap thing.

"Jason Carter, MFD liaison," Jason said and yawned again. "Sorry, long night."

"Thank you for coming."

Jason did that thing when he smiled and winked and showed way too much happy despite being exhausted. Ryan often wished he could channel Jason's eternal happiness.

"You're welcome," Jason said with another smile. "Show me the way."

And like that, Ryan's part in this was over. He watched Jason and Jordan leave to check out whatever pyrotechnics plan they had cooked up, and realized he was standing there like a prize idiot and Jordan was looking back at him and sketching a small wave.

So, Ryan waved back, a thank-you wave—not at all a sexy wave, really—and then he felt even more of an idiot, so he left to find Jay, with his list of concerns in his head.

Jay was in his office, which wasn't exactly *his* office anymore; Adam was sitting on one seat, Micah on the other. From the papers spread out on the desk, they were talking horses, and Ryan didn't really have much to say on that, but he indicated he just needed paper and a pen and wrote out in careful block letters the things he thought needed checking out. Jay mouthed a thank you and placed the paper to one side with a thumbs up.

Ryan moved to leave but stopped when Adam grasped his hand.

"A word?" Adam asked softly and stepped out into the chaos without a jacket.

Ryan immediately went into protective mode, which was his default setting with Adam. After all, Adam had years of missing memories and still suffered from killer headaches. Should he be standing out in the cold? "Everything okay?"

"It's Justin," Adam said, worry in his expression.

"What about him?"

"Something's wrong. He won't talk to me or Ethan, and he's quiet."

"He's always quiet," Ryan said, not because he wanted to play devil's advocate, but because it was the truth. Not only was Justin trained to be stealthy, he also played his cards close to his chest.

Too many secrets.

"No, this is more than normal, and I think it's my fault." Adam tapped his shoulder. "My tattoo. I woke up from a dream that I think could have been memories of the man who did the tattoo, and then I dreamed about being on that ranch and seeing the two men with me die. I mean, I'm not entirely sure, but when I told Justin, he just looked really pained and pale."

Ryan filed away the information. Maybe this was what Justin needed to talk to him about. "I'll talk to him," he reassured Adam.

"There was something else…," Adam murmured, as if he didn't really want Ryan to hear and ask him what it was.

"What?"

"In the dream…." He hesitated again, then couldn't look Ryan in the eyes. "Justin was there in the dreams, front and center."

Too many questions. "I'll talk to him," he repeated. Adam turned to leave, but Ryan stopped him with "Are you okay?"

Adam glanced back, a lost expression on his face, one Ryan had seen many times. "Today isn't a good day, so I gave in and called Ethan. He was coming home anyway, so he's just leaving earlier. I don't like doing it, but I just…"

"Need him," Ryan finished.

"Yeah."

"Is there anything I can do?"

Sometimes Adam was too lost, needed his fiancé by his side, and Ethan was working his notice at the job in Missoula. They hadn't worked out what he would do at Crooked Tree, but Ethan wanted to be with Adam full-time and not just between shifts.

Ryan wished they had the budget at the sheriff's office, but that wasn't happening anytime soon. They had a rookie and that was pretty much all they could afford.

"No, thank you. I'll be okay," Adam said.

And that answered everything. "Good." Ryan ushered Adam back into the warm office, then left.

Justin was waiting for Ryan next to his car, his hands thrust deep into his jacket, a beanie pulled low on his head. "Hey."

Justin always looked so wary, as if, at the drop of a hat, Ryan was going to pull his gun and arrest him or shoot him.

"Hey," Ryan said, and waited for more.

"Is Adam okay? I saw you talking to him."

Ryan considered lying, but Justin wasn't stupid. "He thinks that he remembered something and wanted to talk to me about it."

Justin gave a sharp nod. He was in constant movement from one foot to the other, his expression fixed on Ryan, but Ryan imagined he was aware of every single inch of his surroundings. Whoever trained him way back had done a good job.

"What exactly did he think he remembered?" Justin asked.

"You know I can't divulge information like that."

For the longest time, Justin stared at him, his expression blank. Then he sighed. "Tell me he's okay."

Ryan wished he could say that, wanted to be able to say that he was, but he would be lying. "You should talk to him," he advised, because that was the best he could do.

Justin looked down and kicked at a stone next to his boot. "He won't talk to me. He's avoiding me, or I'm avoiding him, fuck knows." When he returned his gaze to Ryan, there was real grief in his eyes. "He's remembered something and he looks so beaten down. How can I help him?"

That was the most Justin had exposed of himself to Ryan, ever, and part of Ryan, the compassion that wished he could help, wanted desperately to explain that Adam was dealing with memories that made no sense.

He couldn't.

"Find him. Talk to him if you can," Ryan said, and then he added with feeling, "I'm sorry, Justin."

"Not your fault." Justin drew himself tall. "I've got him. I'll do what's best for him." He added, "Always."

If only it was that easy.

They shook hands, and Justin walked back up to Branches.

Justin held too many secrets, and that scared Ryan. Because after today, with what Adam had told him, secrets could destroy Justin and Adam and any friendship they may have.

And likely rip families apart in the process.

Ryan was stopped by Angie, carrying a clipboard and wearing two coats, which he couldn't help but smile at. Her tiny legs sticking out of the bottom of what looked like a large man's coat were quite comical, although he wouldn't say so.

"How are we doing?" she asked, all efficiency and purpose.

"I gave a list to Jay—not a long list," he hastened to add when she frowned. "Concerns that I imagine Jason will notice: access and cables."

She looked at her notes. "Jason, the fireman. Okay, I'll track him down."

And then she was gone. Ryan had almost made it back to his car—part of him not wanting to leave because he was curious to see how all of this worked—when Jordan caught up with him again.

"Hey," Jordan said.

This time Ryan recognized Jordan despite the layers. He had a way of holding himself, all loose-hipped and confident, that was different to Micah.

"Hi."

"You have time for a coffee?" Jordan asked.

Ryan made a show of checking his watch, just because he felt like he had to, even though his morning was booked out here until lunchtime. "More questions?" he asked.

"Yes, kind of."

If he went back to the office, he could clear some paperwork, extend lunch, visit the school... or he could spend a few minutes in the warmth of Branches, maybe get some cake and talk to the intriguing Jordan Darby.

It was an easy decision to make.

CHAPTER 4

~ Jordan ~

Jordan picked a table out of sight from the mess and people outside, and he sat with his back to the room.

They shed coats, gloves, hats, more gloves, and by instinct, Jordan patted his hair down. The damn shortness of it made it stick up at the slightest provocation.

What he was going to ask Ryan was incredibly personal and still a secret to everyone except Micah and Angie.

A woman came to the table. "Morning, Ryan," she said with a big smile. "Mr. Darby."

"Call me Jordan, please."

"What can I get the two of you?"

"The usual," Ryan said and returned her smile. He really did have a lovely smile, his whole face showed his pleasure. "Jordan, this is Ashley."

Jordan stood and extended a hand. "Hello, Ashley."

"I'm Gabe's wife," she said. "We haven't met yet. Not properly, at least."

"Gabe is the middle Todd brother, right? We talked horses with him and Nate?"

"Yep, that's him."

"It's nice to meet you. Everyone has been very friendly." Jordan wanted to make sure she knew that he was relaxing here now he felt better.

"We try. What can I get you Mr.—Jordan?"

"Coffee, and do you do pastries or something? Anything is fine."

She nodded. "No worries, I'll be over in five."

Which left him alone with Ryan, who was examining him curiously.

"What's your usual?" Jordan asked when he couldn't think of a way of launching into what he really wanted to talk about.

"Here?" Ryan evidently hadn't been expecting that question, and for a moment he seemed to need to think about what his usual was. "Black coffee and anything that Ashley has baked today. Doesn't matter what. Chocolate, lemon, pastries, muffins... whatever she does is freaking awesome." Then he subsided into silence and his cheeks flushed pink.

Yes, that could be due to the warmth in here compared to the cold outside, but more likely it was embarrassment. "You take your cake very seriously, then?" Jordan teased.

Ryan mumbled something and then seemed to shrink a little in the chair.

Jordan immediately apologized; he could see discomfort and knew he'd caused it. "Sorry, my sense of humor is shit. Ask my brother."

"I like cake," Ryan blurted and then played with the cutlery on the napkin. "It's my one weakness."

He looked at Jordan and something zapped between them, an awareness of sorts. It sure looked like Ryan was exposing some small part of himself that Jordan felt a kinship to. The way Ryan looked at him, stared at him, the way he was licking his bottom lip. Everything had Jordan sitting forward in his seat.

"You sure don't look like you eat a lot of cake. Do you work out?"

"My brother has a set-up in his garage. I go there."

"Nothing sexier than a man with muscles," Jordan said.

Ryan's mouth parted a little and his eyes widened. Sometimes, Jordan wished there was some kind of gay man's secret handshake or a code word. Too often he flirted with a man who was in no way interested in him. But that there—the eyes, the focus, the way Ryan swallowed—was a signal of sorts. Add in Ryan's gaze lowering to Jordan's lips and back up, and Jordan knew.

He just knew.

"Are you out?" he asked softly.

Ryan nodded and shifted in his seat again, sitting taller. Evidently, he was proud of who he was, and that showed in the way he sat.

Not proud of eating cake, but proud of being out. Got it.

"You?" Ryan asked—no, whispered, in case anyone could overhear if Jordan wasn't.

Jordan appreciated the discretion, even though part of him wanted to write out a banner and stick it in the window. "No," he admitted, "Too much... too many people...." He couldn't find the damn words. Where was a script when he needed one?

"I get that," Ryan said. "Must be hard."

They were interrupted by Ashley coming over with a tray, trailed by a young boy who couldn't have been older than eight, proudly carrying two plates with a selection of cakes on each.

"Hey, Sheriff Ryan," the young boy said with a wide grin that showed a lot of missing teeth.

"Hey, Josh. No school today?"

"The heating broke," Josh announced. "So we get a home day, an' Liam is coming over to see the movie people later. They have cameras and everything."

With the cakes and coffees on the table, Jordan didn't waste time. "These look good." He half turned and looked at Josh, who blinked at him. "Hi, Josh. Come find me when your friend arrives, and I'll give you a tour."

"Wow, hi." The boy wiped his hand on his jeans and held it out, and Jordan shook it very seriously. "My name is Josh," Josh announced. "My mom is here." He waved up at Ashley, who was looking at her son fondly. "I have a sister called Kirsten—she's at college—and my stepdad is Gabe." He scrunched up his nose as if he needed to qualify all of this so that Jordan understood. "Gabe's the brother of Uncle Jay's fiancé, Nate."

"Awesome," Jordan offered, because what did you say to all that excitement and information in one sentence? There was a lot of complicated family up here. He'd only really dealt with Jay and Sam. So at least he now knew that Jay had a fiancé and that Gabe was Josh's stepdad, but he'd lost the thread with the rest.

Didn't matter what he said, though, because Josh was still smiling. "I'm going to go and text Liam. Bye."

Josh left a lot quicker than he'd arrived, and Ashley immediately apologized and thanked Jordan at the same time. "If it's too much, just say so," she tagged on at the end.

"It will be fine. I would love to do it," Jordan admitted. To see the work behind a movie was fascinating to him; to get past the chaos and see the technical side of filming was something he loved to share. To share that with a child as excited as Josh would be something that lifted him out of his still-ill slump.

She thanked him again and left him and Ryan alone.

"He's a good kid," Ryan said, and for a moment, Jordan thought he detected a warning in his tone.

"Seems so." He then concentrated on the plates in front of them. There were tiny bite-size pieces of several different offerings, and he picked up the first one, a quarter of a muffin with the softest, warmest milk chocolate chips inside. Jordan groaned at the taste; he was a sucker for chocolate, and looked up to see what Ryan had tried first.

Ryan hadn't tasted anything; he was just looking at Jordan and seemed to be trying to say something.

Unconsciously, Jordan licked his lips, and fuck, Ryan actually shifted in his seat.

Okay, this was way too intense for him. He needed to rein this in. Then Ryan did something obscenely sexy with his fork and some lemon muffin, and right there and then, Jordan was hard.

All Ryan had done was eat cake.

For a moment, you could hear a pin drop, a frisson of excitement, of expectation.

Then Ryan cleared his throat. "So, you have questions?"

God, yes. Like tell me you're pushy in bed and your thighs are as strong as they look in those regulation pants, and tell me that you really want casual sex with a man who'll be stuck in the closet for at least another four years.

Instead what he said was "I'm writing a script, and I wanted to run some scenarios by you. I wouldn't have to name you, but if you were willing, I could pay you a consultancy fee."

Ryan sipped his coffee and ate another small bite; this time a coffee-walnut slice, like the one Jordan had just finished, that tasted like heaven. Then he sipped some more coffee. "So, you're an actor, you own your own production company, *and* you're a writer?"

Jordan could laugh that off, say something like "sounds like a lot when you put it that way," but he was proud of what he did. "Yes."

"Wow. So, you're not just a pretty face."

Whether Ryan meant that as a compliment or not, Jordan didn't know. Until Ryan flushed scarlet and focused on his plate. Jordan loved that this man wasn't intending to flirt, to come on to Jordan, but he still managed to have Jordan in the palm of his hands.

A hand reached between them and snagged a cake off of Ryan's plate.

"Sam, fuck's sake." Ryan covered his plate with his hands.

"You snooze you lose," Sam teased, then sashayed away with an exaggerated wink back at them.

If it was possible, Ryan was even more scarlet and now utterly incapable of looking at anything other than his plate.

"Sam's a force of nature, isn't he?"

Ryan muttered something like "stubborn," "irritating," and "asshole," in that order. Then he finally looked up. "Yes. I can talk you through some procedures if you want me to."

At this point, Jordan wondered whether he should be honest about the kind of script he was writing. Maybe

Ryan was gay and out but didn't like gay movies or romance.

So instead Jordan just summed up how he felt and then changed the conversation. "Great. We start filming tomorrow, so I'll take your number and we can work out a time. Is that okay, and how tall are you?"

Ryan blinked at the change in conversation. Did the whole "sip, eat cake, sip" thing again.

Jordan realized it wasn't that Ryan didn't want to answer or was deliberately slowing the pace of the conversation. He was just giving himself thinking time.

"Six five," he said. "Why?"

Jordan copied what Ryan had done—coffee, lemon slice, coffee. Then he grinned widely and leaned forward, lowering his voice. "I like my men tall."

Ryan choked on his mouthful of coffee and patted his chest as he sat back in his chair. "Jesus," he snapped. "Is this an LA thing, getting up in my face?"

"Nope," Jordan said gently. "It's a Jordan thing."

Then he left with a soft thank you for Ryan's time. He found himself back in the snow and cold, wishing he'd put his coat and everything else on before stepping outside.

They were going to be here for six weeks. Maybe by the end of that time, he'd be used to the cold.

And possibly he'd have the blushing, sexy sheriff in his bed.

Just for a night.

CHAPTER 5

~ *Adam* ~

Adam woke up.

Suddenly, completely, flailing at the bedclothes that were pinning him down, and shouting for something.

Someone.

Anyone.

"Adam… I've got you… it's a dream…. Adam… I'm here."

The words were on repeat but they meant nothing, just meaningless noise that mixed with the images in his head. Blindly he reached for the notebook he kept by the bed and wrote down the first words he could think of. His hands shook, the book fell to the floor, and he yanked again at the constricting covers, helped and hindered by Ethan, who kept up the litany of reassuring words.

With his feet finally on the floor, Adam attempted to stand, but a head rush had him stumbling.

But it was okay. Ethan was there.

Ethan's always here.

"I've got you," Ethan murmured. "Love you, Adam. I've got you."

Adam pulled away from him; he wanted to stand on his own two feet, sick of these nightmares. Sick of feeling that he was just a step away from recalling everything, only to take a step away from the ghostly memories that teased at his subconscious.

Ethan went straight into post-meltdown care mode, supporting Adam, then helping him to the front room and the wide sofa before handing him water and dropping some headache pills on the table, in case Adam needed them.

Ethan looked after him. Always.

"Can you get my notebook?" Adam asked, his throat tight, his words choked.

Ethan went into the bedroom, came back with the notebook, and handed it straight to Adam, who tucked it down the side of him. He didn't show Ethan what was in it, ever, and Ethan never asked to look. This was personal. Sometimes nothing more than single words or stick figures, sometimes paragraphs of information so detailed that it scared him.

"Sam said he'd be here tomorrow when I need to go back to Missoula," Ethan said as he settled on the sofa next to him. "In case you need him."

"I don't need a babysitter," Adam snapped and then sighed noisily. "Sorry. Shit, my head hurts tonight."

"Can I get you anything?"

Adam wriggled in the seat, never quite getting comfortable, never really falling asleep or relaxing outside of the meditation he did with Justin.

Or that he *had* done with Justin. These last few weeks Justin had been avoiding him, that much was obvious.

"No, I took something, and I'm going to be okay."

"You want to discuss the nightmares?" Ethan always said the same thing, gave Adam the chance to speak about what he was feeling, what he'd seen.

And Adam's answer was always no.

But tonight he could recall some of the images, and he sorted through them in his head and tugged Ethan's hand to him, lacing their fingers. "Maybe," he said. "I spoke to Justin." He coughed to clear the tightness in his throat.

"In the dream?" Ethan asked casually, as if it didn't worry him at all.

"No, for real, and now he's avoiding me."

"What did you talk about?"

Ethan tightened his grip and Adam winced but didn't pull away. Seemed Ethan needed that hold. He'd said a few nights ago that he was afraid that one day Adam would get lost in his dreams and not wake up the same. That must be so freaking scary. How did Ethan cope with feeling like that?

Adam needed to show Ethan the notes he made, talk about the feathery images, blurred around the edges with today's memories, and the mess in his head. "I had a dream about the guy who did my tattoo. His name was Billy Molan and he ran this cool place called Marks and Punctures. I only know that because I googled him," he added before Ethan could ask him if that was a memory.

"What did you remember in the dream?"

"That I knew he was dead, that's all. But Justin was there in my dream, and it all changed, and there was a ranch—not like Crooked Tree, but wide-open spaces—and two men were dead, and Justin was part of everything I was looking at."

"You saw him?"

Adam pulled out the notebook and awkwardly turned pages one-handed until he got to the entry for two weeks ago.

The sketch was simple. Nothing more than a few brushes of pencil and some weird stick figures, but there were names attached to each, and two separate scenes.

"That first one, I don't think I'm there. That's the tattoo place, I think. Google had images of the place and news stories that I checked out after, and it looks like I dreamed. I saw Justin in that dream, but he was off to one side, like he was watching."

Ethan leaned over. "You know that Justin didn't even know you were alive then?"

Adam wouldn't say anything until he'd talked to Ryan, because an insidious suspicion was growing slowly, daily… why would he think of Justin being there, and why was he placing his friend at the center of all his memories?

"Justin didn't say anything, he just looked at me, and there was so much pain in his face, an agony that just floored me."

Ethan pointed to the other picture. "That's the ranch?"

"Two men. Dead. And I'm running."

"And Justin is there?"

Adam pointed at the figure to the left. "Right there."

Ethan hunched over a little. This was his little brother they were talking about, the one who'd killed in the name of some shadowy team that no one knew much about. Justin was out of it now, living with Sam over the restaurant and happy, almost settled. He was still prickly, and sometimes he looked like was going to run, but he stayed with Sam.

"You want me to talk to him?" Ethan asked gently.

"No." Adam didn't have to think about his answer. "God, no. I talked to Ryan, told him about the dreams."

Ethan didn't respond at first.

"You didn't want to talk to me?" he finally asked, sounding hurt.

Adam's head pounded; he wasn't dealing with this very well, and he knew it. "Justin is your brother. I didn't want you to think bad about him, if there was a reason to."

"I can handle it, I'm a cop."

"You love your brother."

"I love you."

They were at a standoff, and then Ethan stood and tugged Adam up. "Let's sleep. We can do this in the morning."

Adam allowed Ethan to lead him, considering that maybe they were going to argue or at least disagree.

Instead, Ethan climbed in and pulled him close, spooning him from behind. "I love you so much, Adam."

"I love you too."

"My heart hurts when yours does."

Adam choked back the tears and instead snuggled back into Ethan's arms. "I'm sorry."

"Don't ever be sorry," Ethan said fiercely. "Ever."

CHAPTER 6

~ *Jordan* ~

The first day of filming was unsatisfying and brutal. The scenes were set-ups for Debbie's character, Mary-Ann, a woman running a ranch on her own, with the added problem of being a widow, having a ten-year-old daughter called Zoe, owning two dogs, and finding orphaned kittens in the snow.

Never let it be said this movie wasn't going to tick all the boxes in cliché Christmas romance.

Jordan's character, Joe, was the traveler who happens on the farm and hides in the barn. Of course, Debbie finds him; he's ill, and she nurses him back to health; he helps her around the farm, the daughter loves him, he and the heroine fall in love, and the kittens get a home.

Yep, calling the leads Mary-Ann and Joe was maybe a step too far, but this script was the only one they could get on short notice, and it was a strong story nonetheless.

"Mary and Joseph," Micah said again, shaking his head in disbelief.

"Mary-Ann and Joe," Jordan corrected him.

They'd taken over one of the cabins in what Crooked Tree called the Forest Area, which was self-explanatory, really, as it backed onto a tangled, gnarly forest of thick pines and banks of snow. Perfect.

The scene they had today was Debbie on the phone with her sister, who was warning her that a storm was coming—cliché #57—and she needed to look after herself. Oh, and was she coming down to the town for Christmas?

"I promise you I'll be there for Christmas Eve. Zoe is super excited, and has hand drawn all these wonderful cards." Debbie delivered her line, and the camera focused in on her pensive expression as she stared out the kitchen window.

Off-camera the actress playing the sister said her bit. "There's nothing stopping you from coming down earlier, sis. You know Zoe would love that."

"I have things to do here. I'll see you in a couple of weeks."

The conversation ends. The camera moved closer, and like the consummate actress Debbie was, her eyes glassed over and a tear rolled down her face. Then she needed to reference the husband who had died and she did so with emotion.

"I miss you, Mark," she said to her reflection, and then closed her eyes.

And pause.

"And cut!" The director, Bob Sterling, a veteran of made-for-TV movies, said decisively. "Perfect, Debs, perfect."

"Thanks, Bob." Debbie wiped away the tears with her hand.

"Who wants to have the kittens?" someone shouted from across the way.

Debbie and Bob grinned at each other. It had been their idea to include orphan kittens. What was better than to add some cute to an already schmaltzy storyline?

"Are you sure about the kittens?" Jordan asked. The idea of wrangling five cats on a set wasn't filling him with enthusiasm.

Until, that was, one of the crew placed a basket on the fake kitchen table and Jordan got his first look at the tiniest creatures imaginable.

"Oh my God." He leaned over for a closer look.

Two blacks, three gray with stripes. All were asleep in one big bundle of fluff. Jordan couldn't help himself, he picked up one of the tiny black kittens and it uncurled in the center of his hand, so small, and gave a soft yawn up at him—and right there and then, Jordan fell in love.

"We need kittens in all our stories," he announced to Micah, who was stroking the kitten's head with the tip of his index finger.

"Yes, boss," Micah said and snorted a laugh.

They fussed over the kittens as the team pulled together the next shot, the morning that Mary-Ann finds Joe in her barn. That was more internal work, and then they were outside working in the barn, which meant moving the shoot across the bridge and up to the secondary location, where it was exposed and freaking cold.

"Why didn't we set this whole movie indoors, with added kittens?" Jordan asked. But he didn't really want an answer, and all he got anyway was Micah chuckling. "You can laugh. I'll be the one in jeans and a light jacket in subzero temperatures."

"That's why you get your name at the beginning of the film, bro," Micah teased.

Emma, the young actress playing Zoe, with her tutor trailing her, stopped at the kittens and couldn't be pulled away. The tutor finally got her to move but not before

Jordan saw the calculating look in Emma's eyes as to how she was going to get to take a kitten home. Her mom was somewhere on set, but didn't strike Jordan as being a push over.

"Eyes up," Micah said, nudging him in the side.

"What?" Jordan glanced at him.

"Tall, dark, and very sexy, heading your way."

Jordan looked in the direction Micah was pointing, and there was Sheriff Carter, looking all kinds of adorable, flushed and really uncomfortable right behind the cameras.

Jordan crossed to him with a smile on his face. "Hey, Sheriff."

"They said it was okay to come in, that you weren't filming."

"No, we're resetting for the next scene."

They stood in silence for a second, and Jordan didn't want that. He could listen to Ryan's voice all day, and he wanted more of it.

"Look," he said, and thrust out his cupped hands and the tiny kitten in them.

"Aww, who's this little fella, then?" Ryan held out a finger, which the kitten mouthed and butted against.

"I don't know. Hang on." He half turned to Micah. "Do the kittens have names?"

Micah shrugged and passed the question back down the line until the answer came that no, there were no names.

"We need to give them names," Debbie said from his side. "What if we write it in as a scene, we could ad-lib and call them, like, Rudolph and whatever. Hi, I'm Debbie."

Debbie not only grinned up at Ryan, but she held out a hand and kind of half hugged the man, who looked over her head right at Jordan, as though he was a deer and Debbie an oncoming truck.

"Nice to meet you," Ryan said formally.

"I'm the lead alongside Jordan."

"Great."

She grinned at him. "You know, the widow and daughter with the ranch, snow, and kittens, and of course the traveler who hides in her barn."

"Great," Ryan repeated. "Sounds good," he added like an afterthought.

Debbie wrinkled her nose at him and then laughed. "It will be with our resident hot leading star here." She thumbed at Jordan, and then took the kitten from him saying that no, Jordan couldn't keep the little tyke.

Which meant that Jordan and Ryan were alone, or as alone as you could be in a mess of technicians trying to make a movie.

"Did you write the script?" Ryan asked, crossing his arms over his chest, then uncrossing them and pushing his hands into the pockets of his sheriff-issue jacket.

"No, but I am a huge fan of Christmas romance," Jordan said, then realized he was coming over as defensive. "Romance in general," he added to qualify the first statement. Then he dipped his head because, jeez, what the hell was he doing? "So, are you here for an official visit?"

Ryan nodded. "Business," he said, but he didn't expand. "Saw Angie, and she said you wanted to talk to me."

"She did?"

Shit. Angie said that? Great, was she matchmaking? Was this something to do with Micah? He turned and searched out Micah, who was watching and freaking well winked at him! That was the shit thing about having a twin; Micah just seemed to know everything about him, just as he knew that Micah was in love with Angie.

"Yes," Ryan continued. "A question about the movie or something I could help with?"

Jordan had to think on his feet, and not focus on how he was going to kill both Angie and Micah.

"Yes, come with me. Least I can do is get you coffee."

Ryan pulled a hand out of his jacket and glanced at his watch. "I have ten minutes."

Jordan smiled up at the big man. "We have cake, and ten minutes is fine."

"I don't *always* eat cake," Ryan blurted, then went scarlet.

Jordan pretended not to notice, but found the reaction so damn cute he had a sugar rush without cake. "Why not? Everyone should eat cake daily."

He led Ryan out of the cabin and across to the large tent holding a mess of boxes, trunks, cables, and chairs. And more importantly, Sam's assistant, Yan, who was in charge of catering down on set.

"Hi, Yan."

"Morning. Coffee?"

"This is Sheriff Carter. He's giving us some technical help, and he loves cake."

"Not all the time," Ryan murmured at his side.

Yan made them coffee and indicated the plates of cake.

"Do you trust me?" Jordan asked as he passed the coffee to Ryan. "With cake, I mean."

Ryan blinked at him and then half smiled. "I don't know. I take it very seriously."

"Go, sit, and I'll bring it over."

Ryan moved to one of the small tables, his breath huffs of white in the cold air. Jordan collected Yan's recommendation and balanced the plates and his mug of steaming caffeine over to the table. He slid in the seat.

"Lemon drizzle. It's Yan's special. He also makes good cookies."

"I'll be the judge of that," Ryan said, and he spoke with a smile.

He took a mouthful, as a wine expert might sip at a glass of Cabernet. He chewed, a thoughtful expression on his face, and swallowed. "That's good."

"So, the reason I wanted to talk to you"—Jordan hoped to hell that his made-up-on-the-spot reason made one lick of sense—"is that we have this drifter, right, and he's ex-Army, rootless after coming back from war. He has this old car, and it broke down, so he walks and ends up in Mary's barn. She'll tell the sheriff, of course."

"Of course." Ryan smiled.

"What would you do?"

Ryan stared at him. "In what way?"

"If a widow with a kid, who you were friends with, told you there was a strange guy in her house, and he was ill, and she didn't know who he was, what would you do?"

"Tell her not to let strangers in the house to start with," Ryan said, all seriousness. "The child is added vulnerability."

"Yeah, but this isn't real life. By the time she comes to talk to the sheriff she's already half in love with the drifter, and her daughter loves him."

"That's dangerous."

"Yeah, but we need to suspend disbelief here."

"Okay, so the sheriff isn't pissed at all?" Ryan asked.

"He is, but he gets over it."

"How?"

"He does a background check, and the guy checks out."

Ryan frowned a little. "Checks out how? A background check will give you arrest records, age, birthplace, all kinds of black-and-white data, but nothing that says 'this is a good guy.'"

"The sheriff would be able to find out if the man was former Army, though?"

"Yes."

"And you'd find the car he says broke down, and tow it somewhere?"

"If we could."

"Okay." Jordan sipped at his coffee. "That gives me something to work with. I need to connect to that in character, persuade her I'm okay, and persuade the sheriff that my intentions are good."

"Yes, and I would need a lot of persuasion."

"Thank you."

Ryan checked his watch again. "I really need to go."

"Sheriff work?"

"Yep."

"I'll walk you out."

Walk him where? To the snow outside? They were a good quarter-mile from the main ranch. *Just to his car, then. He must have driven here.*

Ryan took the empty mugs back to Yan. Jordan wasn't eavesdropping, not deliberately, but he loved that Ryan commented on the cake and the coffee and chuckled at something Yan said back to him.

Ryan really was one of the good guys, and Jordan was so turned on by his voice and his sort of awkwardness, and his height, and his muscles, and just everything about him.

As soon as they rounded the tent, Jordan spotted the sheriff's car, parked neatly under the trees, up against a large bank of snow. He and Ryan would be hidden from view here, at least from the film crew.

"So, the cake was nice." Jordan wanted to make conversation. He'd never had this feeling before, this absolute intention to want to be with someone.

"Yes." Ryan pulled the keys from his pocket.

He was leaving. All he needed to do was get in the car, use the keys, and he'd be gone.

"I still need to talk to you about the procedure in my script," Jordan said a little desperately.

Ryan tilted his head. "You were going to text me a time."

"Friday. I'll come to your place. There's no peace here."

Ryan smiled ruefully. "It's not exactly quiet at my place either. But okay. Head through town, find Carter's, and ask for me at the bar."

"You live in a bar? I mean, at a bar."

"Family business. And over the bar, actually."

"Seven okay? Maybe eight? You want me to bring takeout?"

"No, I'll sort it. You like Italian?"

Jordan could imagine reaching up, tangling his hands into Ryan's chestnut hair, pulling him down for kisses... he wondered what Ryan would taste like. Would he want Jordan to take control of the kiss, or would he be the one who pressed Jordan back against the car and took his fill?

Fuck, this is turning me on.

"I love Italian," he said. Then Ryan was in the car, with no kisses, no touches, and Jordan was waving goodbye, a little lamely.

At least he had Friday.

So, he went back to filming. He got there just in time to watch Debbie nail her interaction with the kittens and think that right there was Christmas romance movie gold.

CHAPTER 7

~ *Ryan* ~

Ryan felt unsettled for the rest of the day.

There had been something in Jordan's expression and the way those amazing, stormy eyes kept focusing on Ryan's lips that made him want to lean in and kiss the man senseless.

Whatever Ryan thought about himself—that he was too tall, too big, too soft in the middle, too much a sheriff, too... everything that other men didn't want—it seemed like Jordan wanted to get something going while he was here.

Jordan was in the closet, so it wasn't like it would be permanent. Ryan had had enough shit in his life after coming out to even consider hiding the man he eventually fell in love with.

But Ryan could maybe go for a couple weeks of sex. He kind of wanted sex.

Sex with Jordan. *Yep.*

Then he recalled Jordan's comments about how Ryan should google his family. He didn't say it like he was worried what Ryan would find, just that maybe it was a complicated story played out in public life, as if he was tired of telling the same thing over and over.

Google was Ryan's friend. In the space of an hour, he'd seen more than enough photos of Jordan shirtless, several of which appeared to be made up of Jordan's head pasted onto someone else's body. He'd also found links to stories about Jordan, which he'd followed, and just as many on Micah.

Turned out Jordan and Micah had been child stars, first as "baby one" and "spare baby" on a soap opera their dad, Mitchell Darby, had starred in, and then in a Disney series where they played twins. That had been quite successful, garnering attention and a whole slew of fans, some of whom had websites they'd set up, none of which were being updated now. From the dates of the last posts, the popularity of Jordan and Micah as teenage heartthrobs had ended a while back.

When the show ended with the stars leaving for college in the storyline, Micah had stopped acting altogether, preferring to work behind the scenes. Jordan, on the other hand, went on to star in a couple of Hollywood movies, neither of them big, and then settled into made-for-TV versions, mostly romances set at Christmas.

"The King of Christmas is back in his seventh film," one of the links announced, and Ryan clicked through to the article. This was last year's Christmas movie, in which Jordan wore a soldier's scarlet uniform as heir to the throne in a made-up European country. At least, Ryan hadn't heard of the country, so he guessed they'd invented it. There was a link to something called the *Internet Movie Database*, so he clicked on that, and it brought up a list of the things Jordan had acted in. Yep, seven Christmas films, all romances; the two movies, then the series before with Micah. It didn't look to Ryan like Jordan had much time off since he was born. He must really love his job to never stop working.

Ryan moved on to Wikipedia, which was a lot more revealing. The twins were born in December 1985, which made them thirty—three years younger than Ryan. The twins had lost their father when they were young—cancer, it looked like—and both their mom and dad had their own Wiki pages. At that point he didn't want to click anywhere else; somehow it felt like an invasion of privacy, and that was an odd feeling given investigation was what he did for a living.

A knock on his door interrupted his thought process, and before he could say anything, his brother Saul barged into his room. Ryan shut his laptop so quickly that he knew damn well what it looked like.

Saul held up his hand and began backing out of the room with a muttered "Oops, sorry to interrupt your alone time."

"Asshole, I was looking at Wiki."

Saul frowned. "Wiki does porn now?" he deadpanned.

"No, Wiki doesn't do—Jeez, what do you want?"

"Eddie and the kids are downstairs."

Ryan immediately stood, placing his laptop on the table and striding to the door. "What happened?"

Saul stopped him with a hand to his arm. "Nothing. They were shopping for school clothes and decided to drop in. Calm down."

"The kids are okay?"

"Yes."

"And Eddie?"

"Yes, jeez, Ry, he's just visiting."

Eddie, the second-oldest brother, never *just* visited. He was the only one of the five who'd been married, the only one who had kids, and the only one who couldn't handle either. Of course, his first wife, Sarah—or, as Ryan liked to call her, Hell-Wife—had done a number on Eddie, but still, he was an idiot in general, the bane of Saul's life. Eddie had always been in trouble, ever since he was small, and he relied way too much now on Saul and Ryan to provide a free babysitting service.

Not that he or Saul minded, but they weren't going to tell Eddie that.

Eddie visiting at five in the evening probably meant the kids hadn't eaten dinner, and for a second, Ryan thought about where to take them, but Saul was one step ahead of him. When Ryan reached the bottom of the stairs, Milly and Jake were sitting at the kitchen table with orange juice and the smell of cooking pizza filling the space around them.

"Uncle Ryan!"

Jake saw him first, and Ryan had the little boy climbing him like he was a tree, finally winding his arms around Ryan's neck and holding tight. He was only four, and Ryan could easily hold his weight while Milly swung off his hand, chattering on about a dance at school and how she was learning all her spellings.

No sign of Eddie. Ryan glanced at Saul, who inclined his head to the door to the bar. Seemed Eddie wasn't coming in here.

Not again.

Ryan waited until both kids were back at the table pulling apart the hot pizza and talking to Saul, and then he casually pushed open the door to the bar.

Eddie sat slumped at the bar, nursing a glass filled with amber liquid. If Eddie had turned to alcohol, this was more serious than Ryan had imagined.

"Hey," Ryan said and slid onto the stool next to Eddie.

"'M not gonna drink it," Eddie said, his voice scratchy and low. "It's a test."

Eddie was four years sober—did he test himself a lot? Ryan reached over and took the whiskey away, going behind the bar and taking out two Cokes. He slid one to Eddie and kept the other for himself.

"What's up, E?"

"She left me, said it was all too much, wanted to go out partying, wasn't ready to settle down."

Shit. "I'm sorry." For all his brotherly need to get a background check on Eddie's girlfriend, Jenny, she had seemed quite nice. He guessed she wasn't if she wanted to party when it was clear Eddie was a recovering alcoholic with two small children.

Eddie nodded, and took a big swallow of the Coke. "The kids loved her, and they said goodbye this morning, and she hugged them, and then when they were on the school bus, she began to pack." He looked up right at Ryan.

Eddie looked like shit. Closer inspection in the dim bar light exposed his red-rimmed eyes and defeated expression.

"What did the kids say?"

"They don't know. I haven't told them yet."

"You want me to—"

"No, jeez, I didn't come here for Saint Ryan to sort out my freaking kids." Eddie pushed back his stool and made to leave.

Ryan grabbed his hand. "I'm sorry, sit down. I just meant if you needed help."

Eddie struggled for a second, but he was the shortest of the brothers. Ryan was bigger and stronger, and even with the bar in the way, he had the upper hand. Finally, Eddie just sat back down.

"Talk to me." Ryan moved to sit next to Eddie again.

"Jake called her Mom and she freaked out, I could see it. She hugged them goodbye, like she does every day, and he said 'Bye, Mom.' She went really pale, and she wouldn't talk to me." He reached into his pocket and pulled out a velvet box. "I was going to ask her to marry me."

"Eddie, I'm sorry."

Eddie looked at Ryan then, his expression bleak. "I loved her. No, I love her."

"Then why are you still sitting here? Go talk to her."

Eddie blinked. "I know you all think I'm useless, but Milly and Jake come first in everything."

Ryan gave him a sideways hug. Whatever his faults, Eddie was a good dad when it mattered. "She may have just panicked. Talk to her, at least do that."

"Can I—"

"Yes, the kids can stay here. We'll have a sleepover, and you can explain you're a package deal and that you love her. Don't come back empty-handed."

Eddie left his stool, and this time Ryan didn't stop him, waiting until he disappeared out the front door before returning to the kitchen. The children were covered in red sauce and laughing loudly at Saul doing something with the lettuce from the crisper. Ryan saw the lettuce had eyes made of tomatoes.

"Guess what, kids," Ryan said, injecting huge uncle-enthusiasm into his voice, "who wants to build a blanket fort and sleep over!"

Saul shot him a quick look, but Ryan shrugged. The kids had stuff here permanently because Eddie's job in security sometimes had him working overnight. Ryan wanted Eddie to be happy, wanted Jenny to be the one. And tonight, he had uncle duties to perform.

"Can we have hot chocolate?" Jake asked.

"And popcorn!" Milly demanded.

Only when Ryan was in the blanket fort with Jake fast asleep on his chest did he question the wisdom of sleeping on the floor.

"I love your tummy. It's all soft." Milly pressed her pointed chin into his middle. "And I love you, Uncle Ryan."

"I love you too, pumpkin."

She looked sideways up at him. "Do you think Jenny will come back?"

So much for secrets about what had happened to Jenny. One thing Ryan had learned from being an uncle was that kids saw straight through most of the handy lies that adults told them. "I hope so," he finally said.

"Me too. I liked her. She made Daddy smile."

Ryan's heart cracked just a little.

The door to the fort was swept aside and Saul appeared bearing coffee in travel mugs. "Can anyone come in?" he asked.

He crawled into the tiny space left and lay on his back staring up at the bottom of the dining room table, which formed the solid main structure. Milly hugged close to her uncles, and her breathing soon settled to sleep rhythm.

"Think Eddie will be okay?"

Ryan sighed. "I hope so."

"He loves that girl. The kids do as well. I really thought, after everything Sarah did to him and the kids, that he could be the one of us to be happy and settled."

Ryan huffed. "That's a depressing thought."

"Well, you got yourself a boyfriend yet?"

There were many ways Ryan could answer that. Instead he looked sideways at his brother and decided to be honest. "Not at the moment, no."

They lay in silence awhile. Then "This shit isn't good for my back," Saul groused.

"Suck it up, old man."

"The things I do for my brothers."

Ryan smiled. "And we love you for it."

Saul elbowed him. "Yeah, you'd all better love me forever, then."

All the things Saul had given up, the family he could have had if he wasn't being a dad to his brothers, the life he could have lived... Ryan, Eddie, Jason, and Aaron, they all knew what he'd done. What he still did.

"Love you," Ryan murmured.

But Saul was already asleep, curled up on his side like a pretzel.

Ryan willed himself to sleep, but it wasn't happening straightaway. All he could think was that at some point this week he was meeting up with Jordan, and wouldn't it be good if maybe they acted on the spark of attraction between them.

What a slim, sexy, and very pretty actor would want with a man like him, he didn't know, and he laid a hand on his belly. He wasn't carrying excess weight; at six four he could carry off all the cakes he could eat. Still, he would be willing to bet that under Jordan's clothes were a whole bunch of muscles.

Maybe that was what in-the-closet actors did? They found the nearest gay guy on location and had a couple of weeks of fun.

Ryan prided himself on being a catch; he had a steady job, a heart that needed someone badly, and so much love inside him just waiting for the right man.

Unlikely it would be Jordan, but attraction and a few weeks of flirting on the down-low? He was okay to go for that.

No need to get his fragile, needy heart involved at all.

CHAPTER 8

~ *Justin* ~

Justin watched Sam sleep for the longest time. He was one of those guys who despite being short somehow managed to stretch from one side of the bed to the other. They'd made love tonight, and true to form, Sam had collapsed on the bed and not moved thereafter except to sprawl about.

Justin hadn't found it as easy to sleep, so he sat on the windowsill, looking down at the snow below and the tent village that proved they weren't alone at Crooked Tree.

Sam moved in his sleep, muttered something, and Justin turned back to see him reach over to Justin's pillow and pull it close to him to hug, and all Justin could do was smile. He loved Sam to distraction, to the point that he could almost forget everything in his past. Sam did that: he balanced Justin and made him a better man for it.

"Come back to bed," Sam muttered, his eyes open and looking right up at Justin.

Justin smiled down at him and crossed to the bed, kneeling at the side. "There's no room," he teased.

Sam frowned and then bodily moved back to *his* side and lifted the covers. Justin slid in without argument and scooted back, happy to be the little spoon until the warmth of Sam against his scarred back became too much. Normally after about ten minutes.

"Talk to me," Sam said.

"What about?"

"Justin, fuck's sake, about whatever is making you prowl around half-naked in the middle of the night."

"Oh, it's nothing, really."

Except it was, it was the biggest everything he could imagine, and it could end with him and Sam having to leave Crooked Tree.

"Bullshit," Sam snapped without heat, his tone playful.

"I spoke to Ryan today, asked if maybe we could talk about the events Adam is starting to recall. Memories I'm a part of."

"From when you disappeared?"

"No, from the murders when he was in WITSEC."

Sam held him tight briefly and then moved to straddle him, before rolling them sideways and holding him close. He pressed a kiss to Justin's throat. "You didn't even know Adam was alive then, so you didn't have anything to do with all that."

Justin carded his hands in Sam's hair. "So trusting," he said. "It doesn't matter what questions you have, you just accept I'm a good man."

Sam huffed a breath, warm on Justin's skin. "You told me everything you could, and I love you."

"Sam?"

"Hmmm?"

Sam was falling asleep splayed over him, but Justin had one more thing to ask. "What if I had to leave Crooked Tree?"

There was no hesitation. "I'll go where you go. I'd find someone to cover my role at Branches, because it's always good to have a fallback financially for us. Maybe hire in a manager, but it would be okay."

"I love you," Justin said after a moment's pause.

More than life itself. More than being home. More than anything.

"I love you too," Sam murmured, his breath hot against Justin's throat.

"Will you come with me when I talk to Ryan?"

"Will you tell him anything I don't already know?"

"Just the dreams... and what Adam is recalling. I want him to remember everything but it might mean we'd have to leave to give him space."

"And I said that was okay. And, of course I'll come with you."

"I love you."

"And I love you."

And then Sam's breathing evened out and he was asleep over Justin, like a blanket.

Finally, pressed down into the mattress like that, Justin slept.

Justin sent the text as soon as he was awake, Ryan responded quickly, and a meeting was scheduled. Only when he and Sam were in the car on the way to the sheriff's office did nerves start to grate inside him. He felt edgy and hot, and not even Sam's hand on his knee was helping.

"Calm down," Sam encouraged.

"I can't," Justin bit out, irritation and anger curling in his gut. If it were that simple, he'd have done it already! He closed his eyes, listened to the noise of the road, attempting to center himself, but nothing was working.

The car slowed, crunching over gravel, and stopped.

Sam twisted in his seat. "Seriously, Justin, calm down."

Calm down? How the hell was he going to calm down? He was basically handing himself over to the sheriff, and he was going to give Ryan permission to be honest with Adam. "I'm trying," he said and gritted his teeth.

Sam looked at him, all concerned and sympathetic, and Justin didn't care where they'd stopped, he shoved open his door and stepped into the snow piled at the side of the road, right up to his knees.

Sam rounded the car before he'd even moved an inch. "Justin?"

"Fuck off, Sam. You don't know what I did, you don't know what I saw, the choices I made. If I told you half of what I've done, you'd leave me here in the snow. I don't understand why the hell you're even with me, let alone allowing me to fuck you." The words tumbled out of him in a slew of self-hatred and guilt, but all Sam did was look at him steadily, as if he didn't care.

"Why don't you care?" Justin snapped, aware his jeans were getting damp.

Sam looked at him, not moving his gaze. His expression was still the same, compassion written in every line of him.

"I'm not any good for you!" Justin was shouting now. "I try really hard to be normal, but it doesn't work all the time. And then I yell at you, and you never once push back, and all you do is fucking *smile* at me like it's all okay. Well, I'm telling you now, it's not okay, and when you listen to what I tell Ryan, you'll be running out of that room." The shouting was louder, but just getting the words out there, the fears he kept locked inside, made him feel impossibly light. If Sam would just leave him, then Justin wouldn't have to care that what he'd done could hurt him.

Sam crossed his arms over his chest and paused, evidently waiting for something else. Then he said softly, "Are you done now?"

And abruptly, Justin *was* done. His jeans were soaked, his feet frozen, his heart lighter, and his head clearer. "Well, shit," he muttered.

Sam sighed and gestured at the snow up to Justin's knees. "Get in the car, Justin."

Justin did as he was told, feeling more embarrassed than he had in a long time.

Sam turned on the engine, and adjusted the heating so it was on Justin's legs. Then, in a smooth move, he yanked Justin his way and kissed him long and hard. "Mine," he said.

That single word went straight to Justin's cock and he groaned low in his throat. Sam had the ability to get right inside him and tip him over into unknown territory, just using the look of utter determination in his gorgeous eyes.

They didn't talk for the five minutes it took to pull into the sheriff's office, but as soon as the car stopped, Justin leaned over for a kiss.

"Sorry," he mumbled against Sam's lips.

In answer, Sam simply deepened the kiss. When he pulled away, he was smiling. "Let's do this thing."

"You brought cakes," Ryan joked, taking the container and looking around as if considering where to put it, finally clearly deciding it was best off in his office, which he showed them straight into. The sheriff's station wasn't big, maybe six or so rooms ranged around an inquiry desk staffed by the inimitable Frankie McAllister.

"Have a seat." Ryan indicated the circle of comfy chairs ranged next to his immaculate desk. Sam sat near the door, Justin to his left, and Ryan settled his large frame opposite.

Justin didn't hesitate. "Adam finally said something to me, told me he wasn't sleeping, that he was dreaming all the time. I didn't know what to say, so I asked him what he was dreaming about. In these dreams he was seeing things that he shouldn't know, seeing things that weren't even possible."

Ryan eased forward in his seat, elbows on his knees, his hands clenched between them. "What kind of things? Memories?"

"He told me he saw the two agents killed at the ranch he worked at when he was in witness protection. But he couldn't have."

Ryan considered. "How do you know that? As far as I was aware, you didn't even know Adam was still alive, so how can you know what he did and didn't see?"

Justin reached into his jacket pocket, closing his hand around the memory stick that was one of three copies he had. He didn't pull it out yet; he had to make Ryan see what he was trying to achieve. "There's more. He's placing me at the scene in his dreams."

Ryan sat upright. "He saw you? You were actually there?"

Justin swallowed. What he was doing here was huge, but he owed this to Adam. Next to him, Sam placed a hand on his knee, reassuring, comforting.

"That was my job," Justin said. "I didn't know…." He trailed away and paused. "My partner, Rob, was supposed to work it, but we had to go to contingency when he was caught in a mess in DC."

"So what you're saying, in my office, is that you admit you killed the two men on duty who were protecting Adam."

That wasn't a question from Ryan, it was a flat statement of fact, and Justin's chest tightened. "No, I'm admitting nothing. In fact, that's one thing I didn't do."

He'd done what he'd done and there was no going back, and he liked Ryan. He hated to destroy the illusion that he was some kind of antihero, that somehow there were reasons for what he did. At that time, he'd thought he was working for the good old US of A, but he'd been lied to, fucked over, and hung out to dry. He'd been wrong, and he'd done some awful things that he needed to come to terms with.

"The thing is, I wasn't there to take *them* out," he said. What he said next was going to wreck everything, but he didn't need to say a word because Ryan closed his eyes.

"Fuck, Justin," Sam said on a gasp of disbelief. "You were sent to kill Adam?"

"James Mahone—Jamie, that was the name he was using. And I didn't know it was Adam. Shit, as far as I knew Adam was dead years before, okay? I got there and the two guys were already dead." He pressed his fingers to his brow. "Straight to the head, execution-style. I did a cursory look, had to leave. I could recognize my boss's work, so I knew it was something to do with my team, but it wasn't me. Hell, if Adam had been there…." He paused, the words choked up in his throat. "If he was there, hiding, watching, I didn't see him. But what he says he remembers is me front and center killing those two men."

Ryan pursed his lips, his dark eyes holding so many questions, and all Justin could think was that now was the right time. He pulled out the memory stick.

"If Adam is remembering, then there might be a time when you can tell him it all much better than I can, away from emotion and just giving him cold, hard facts. This gives you everything you need."

Ryan took the proffered stick and turned it over in his hands. "What will I find on here?"

"Names, dates, everything I could get before I blew up the computer. God knows what is out there in the cloud, I can't believe for one minute I am the only one with this information. If Adam is starting to recall facts, then he could need your support. There's proof in there that I wasn't the shooter he saw, but it won't matter to him at the moment if I tell him that. Because he has these images in his head from the dreams and he'll need it from an official source, like you."

"Justin—"

"I know it's a big favor to ask, Ryan, but I wanted this in your hands, so if something happens to me, and if you need to…." He hunched a little, and Sam's hand tightened on his knee.

"I was going to say," Ryan began, pulling the conversation away from Justin's fears, "if you told Adam the truth, I'm convinced he would believe you."

"There'll always be doubt in his mind, and in Ethan's. I've seen the way my brother and Adam look at me at times." Emotion choked him, and he hated that he couldn't get the words out right. "I don't want them to look at me and hate me. I hate myself enough for everyone."

"Stop it, Justin," Sam snapped from his side.

Justin ignored him, focusing instead on Ryan. "If it comes to it, if they lose what little respect they have for me and there's reason to—" He looked at Sam, who still looked pissed but nodded at the unspoken question.

That was one thing Justin could believe in. Whatever he'd done, whoever he'd once been, he had Sam in his life. And Sam loved him.

"I'll leave. I'm not serving time for what I've done. I'll leave and find the most distant point where it will be as if I'm dead."

Ryan shifted in his seat. "What if you deserve to go to prison?"

"Fuck, Ryan—" Sam began, but Justin stopped him talking.

"I already am. In my head, I live with it every day. But if you think… if you feel that Adam would be better off with me facing some kind of justice?" He stopped, couldn't say any more, and Sam gripped his hand so tight he was cutting off circulation.

"Justin did what he did for his country," Sam said firmly. "Whatever lies he was told, whoever he was supposed to kill, he lives with it every day."

"I know," Ryan said, his body language about as far from hostile as you could get. "I guess I'm playing devil's advocate here. Playing the what-if game."

"We'll go and start a life somewhere else if it comes to it," Justin said. "Sam and I will go, and you will have what you need to blow the whole thing up."

Ryan hesitated momentarily and turned the stick over and over in his hand. "You know I should escalate this. It's my duty to do that."

Justin nodded. "Our families have been friends a long time, Ryan. I hope you can sit on this for me because of that and in spite of the fact you're the sheriff. I trust you."

Ryan avoided answering that. "What will you do now?"

"Adam needs space to recall things on his own. It's like some days he can't even look at me."

That wasn't exactly an answer but Ryan inclined his head in acknowledgment. "So, you plan on leaving anyway?"

"For the summer, maybe, just to give him space." He glanced sideways at Sam.

Sam had a business, a career, an investment in Crooked Tree. It would be difficult for him to leave with Justin. Maybe this was something Justin needed to do on his own.

"I'll be with him," Sam said, his tone allowing for no discussion on the matter. Justin's chest tightened with emotion and he thought he was going to cry.

Fucking stupid emotions.

He coughed to clear his throat. "Ryan, will you sit on this information unless you need to release it, for Adam's sake?"

Ryan gazed at him, his expression thoughtful, and then gave a sharp nod. "Yes. For Adam." Then he added in a much softer voice, "And for you."

Justin and Ryan stood, and Ryan was the first to pull Justin in for a hug. Something passed between them, an understanding, and Justin hoped to hell Ryan could feel his regret.

Outside, back in the parking lot, Sam sat very still in the car, both hands on the wheel. He stared out at the snow swirling around them. This was probably one of the last snowfalls of the year until late fall, and it simply added another inch to the already deep piles.

"Where would we go?" Sam asked.

"If we had to?" Justin asked, to clarify.

Sam nodded and then side-eyed him. "Somewhere with snow still, right? Where Christmas is white."

"And where there's a summer just like here," Justin pointed out.

Sam started the car. "Let's hope it doesn't come to that."

"I love you. Every part of me loves you," Justin's voice held so much emotion that it obviously cut deep into Sam.

Choked with his own emotion, Sam smiled gently. "Every part of me loves you too."

CHAPTER 9

~ *Jordan* ~

Jordan pulled up outside Carter's. The place was easy to find mostly because of its big neon sign and was clearly popular. Cars filled the parking lot, and he parked on the end of one of the lines.

As he made his way through rows of vehicles, he looked up at the sign and took in as much information as he could before he went inside. He couldn't fail to see the rainbow in the window and wondered if that was just some kind of random window dressing or Ryan's influence. If Ryan's family owned the place and he was out, then they'd want to acknowledge that, he supposed.

When he stepped inside, he knew immediately what he was walking into.

He saw a couple of men at the bar, one with his arm around the other. Next to them two women sat holding hands and talking. Groups of people were dining, some of them families. Looked like this place was somewhere that accepted everyone.

He made his way to the bar. The man standing behind it had to be related to Ryan; he was older and had silver at his temples and more years carved into his face, but his smile was Ryan's and he had the same dark eyes. Maybe this was Ryan's father.

"Hi." Jordan leaned over the bar.

"What can I get you?" the older man asked.

"I think I'm here to see your son," Jordan said. "Ryan."

"I don't have any children."

"Oh. But Ryan lives here?"

"He does."

Getting a straight answer out of this guy is like getting blood from of a stone, Jordan thought. "Can you, um…."

"You said you only *think* you're here to see him?"

"I did?"

This was getting confusing. Then the man broke into a wide grin and extended a hand, which Jordan took.

"Just fucking with you. I'm Saul, Ryan's oldest brother. He's upstairs. Go through the back door, turn right, take the stairs, and his door is the first one." He released Jordan's hand. "Take these with you." He handed over two beers and a bottle of wine.

"What do I owe you?" Jordan moved to pull out his wallet.

"Nothing." Saul waved him away. "Get yourself upstairs. And comment how tidy it looks, okay?"

"Okay." Jordan gave an answering smile and pointed at the door. "That door?"

"Yep. Nice to meet you."

"And you."

Jordan wasn't lying; it was nice to see someone connected to Ryan. It wasn't as though Jordan could google Ryan and get all the details of his family or his background, not like Ryan could do with him.

He went through the door, which opened onto a large internal hallway and the stairs, which he took two at a time, excitement in every step, until finally he was outside the door. He shifted the three bottles to one arm and knocked. The door opened really quickly.

"Hey," Ryan said and widened the door.

He looked good. Just as good out of uniform as in it. Tonight he was in jeans that stretched over muscled thighs, a slim black tee that hugged every muscle, and he'd done something to his hair—maybe gel or something, whatever. He looked edible.

Something was definitely going to be happening tonight.

"Hey, your brother gave me these," Jordan said and held out the wine and the two beers. "I called him your dad. He didn't seem to mind, though, so I don't think I fucked up too bad."

Ryan took the bottles and walked over to a small kitchen, no more than a breakfast bar, really, with a microwave and a kettle. Maybe he didn't do a lot of cooking.

"Beer or wine?" Ryan asked. "Dinner's in twenty. I made something instead of getting take out."

"You cooked?"

"Simple stuff, in the downstairs kitchen. Lasagna, so beer or wine?"

"Wine is good," Jordan said.

He crossed to a shelving unit against the wall and looked at some of the photos there. He spotted five men in a row in one picture, and he could make out Saul at one end and Ryan at the other. Three men, all with a similar look to them, stood in the middle. The five weren't ranged by height; Ryan was easily the tallest and had the nicest smile.

Or am I just biased?

"My brothers. Left to right, in order of age. Saul, you met him downstairs, then Eddie. Aaron—he's the paramedic—Jason, the fireman you met on set, and then me."

"So, where did you get the tall genes from?" Jordan asked. Not that the other brothers were short, probably all hitting six foot, but Ryan was definitely taller.

"My dad's family, or so Saul tells me. Dad's cousins were tall. They live in Canada now, we don't really see them; some kind of family falling out."

Jordan considered pressing for more, but he sensed the story might be too much for what he was pretending was an evening to talk about his script.

Ryan went on anyway. "And this is my niece and nephew, Milly and Jake. They're Eddie's children and spoiled because so far, Eddie's the only one of us to have kids."

"Really?"

"Yeah, Saul always said he'd had enough bringing us up, and Aaron and Jason just haven't found the right person."

"What about you?"

"Me?" Ryan frowned. "No, I don't have kids."

"No, I mean, do you want them?" He couldn't believe he'd asked that and even began to create a sentence whereby he apologized, but Ryan beat him to it.

"One day," Ryan offered. "I'm thirty-three. I guess I should be doing something about it soon."

Jordan's heart swelled; he could imagine Ryan holding a baby. He had to school his features into a mask of faint interest without thinking that his own wanting kids was a good match for Ryan. Yes, he wanted kids, three or four of them. *One day.*

"I'm thirty," he said.

Ryan smiled at him. "Just a baby," he teased.

"Old enough." Jordan offered a wink as punctuation to that. Then, when he realized he was an idiot, he concentrated on sipping his glass of wine.

"Did you bring the script with you?"

"Do you have a laptop? I have it on a stick."

Ryan walked through a side door that Jordan assumed led to a bedroom. Part of him, the part that wanted to climb Ryan and get off against him, felt like following him. After all, there was definitely something between them; all it needed was for one of them to say something and they'd be off.

Ryan came out, opening the laptop as he walked and clicking buttons before passing it to Jordan.

Jordan placed his wine on a coaster and then balanced the laptop, pushing in the stick, locating the file, opening it, and handing the whole thing to Ryan.

No one else had read what he'd written, not even Micah. Because hell, Micah might have signed off on the five year plan, but Jordan wasn't ready to share the script just yet. He didn't think Micah would be dismissive of the story he was writing, but could they take the chance on something that might not be a commercial success?

Ryan shut the laptop and placed it on the coffee table in front of the huge comfy-looking sofa and straightened. "Dinner first," he announced. "Then I can read it properly."

"You don't have to read it tonight."

"I want to. Dinner is in the main shared kitchen downstairs. We should have the place to ourselves."

Jordan followed Ryan out of the room and down another set of stairs, which opened out into a large brightly lit kitchen. The scents of garlic and tomato hit him as they entered and his mouth watered. Whatever was cooking had an Italian smell to it, and he loved Italian food.

"Hope you like lasagna. I didn't ask if you were vegetarian, so I did two, just in case."

"No, I like meat," Jordan said, then winced internally when Ryan raised an eyebrow.

So, it was going to be *that* kind of evening. Hell, he could do innuendo with the best of them. He sidled up to Ryan and leaned over the piping hot lasagna. "What can I do?"

"The salad is in the refrigerator if you want to get it, and I'll take some more wine. I'm not on duty tomorrow, and I can always go into the bar and get more if we empty that one."

"You looking to get me drunk, Sheriff?" Jordan teased.

"Obviously."

Once the plates were filled, they sat at the table opposite each other. Jordan was too hungry to delay eating. The sauce was hot, the pasta perfect, the salad fresh, the wine soft, and Ryan was sitting there looking all kinds of gorgeous.

Ryan cleared his throat. "How is filming going?"

"Fine. We're clearing all the exterior scenes next—me in a shirt and no jacket in the snow." Jordan couldn't help the shudder; Montana was freaking cold.

"Any night shoots?"

"Some. We have packs we can use to keep warm. I just hope I can deliver all my lines without my teeth chattering."

"Did you always want to be an actor?"

Oh, now that was a leading question, and he had a standard answer: he was born to love it, acting was in his genes, and he was happy all the damn time. But somehow, he wanted to be completely honest with Ryan.

"I was born into it. I assume you googled me?" He waited for Ryan's cautious nod. "Well, Dad was an actor on a soap opera as you no doubt read, and we—Micah and I—were the babies they switched about to play his newborn son in the show. As twins we could do that, one of us asleep, the other awake, taking turns. We worked on that set until we were six or so. Then I had a few years of small bit parts until Micah and I landed our main show, where we played twins."

"No surprise there," Ryan said.

"Yeah. It ran ten seasons. I can't say I always wanted to be an actor, though. Not like a normal kid wants to be an astronaut or a sports icon. I just *was* an actor."

"So, you don't enjoy it?" Ryan looked horrified, as though he couldn't understand someone doing a job they didn't really love.

"I love it now. I think I burned out with the Jordan-Micah show, and Micah decided he'd had enough. I kept my hand in with other things: small parts in movies, voice-over for a Disney film, that kind of thing. I never lost the focus on acting, and then, of course, the Christmas movies happened."

"The King of Christmas."

Ryan forked up another mouthful of salad. The dressing left a small smear on his bottom lip and he darted his tongue out to collect it, which had Jordan squirming a little in his seat. Ryan wasn't even trying to be provocative, but he had Jordan half-hard in a freaking kitchen over dinner.

"I'll never escape that title," Jordan said, and concentrated on cutting through layers of pasta, meat, and sauce.

"I read that your films are the most-watched made-for-TV movies."

"A lot of that is down to my co-stars." Jordan never took all the credit for anything and always acknowledged the team around him.

"So, tell me more about the script."

Jordan delayed the inevitable by asking for more lasagna and watching the muscles bunch in Ryan's forearm as he scooped out another serving. He had very sexy forearms with a dusting of hair; his skin tone was warmer than Jordan would have expected given the cold and snow and the long Montana winters. Idly, Jordan considered how hairy Ryan might be elsewhere: was he smooth to touch or did he have chest hair that would crinkle under Jordan's touch? Was he the kind of guy to manscape, did he have a treasure trail leading south to his—

"Earth to Jordan."

He snapped out of his inappropriate thoughts about body hair and snapped back to Ryan. "Sorry?"

"You want more salad with that? I can make some more."

"No, thank you."

They continued to eat, and Jordan tried his very hardest not to stare right at Ryan, but it was hard. His eyes were so dark and he had this way of looking up at Jordan, with a soft smile just at the right moment. He seemed almost shy.

Jordan loved that.

Only when he couldn't eat another thing and had pushed his empty plate to one side did he begin to explain about the script. At least he began to, until he remembered he had something else to say.

"Dinner was wonderful," he began. "Do you cook a lot?"

Ryan finished his own second helping with the final mouthful, chewed, swallowed, then picked up his wine.

"Saul did all the cooking when we were growing up, by the time I was old enough to know he cooked for us he was doing all the right things. Eddie, he's the second oldest, he said dinner started off with a lot of mac 'n' cheese for us all. Saul was only eighteen when he was thrust into having to look after four brothers. Eddie was ten, Aaron seven, Jason six, and I was just a baby. Saul had to learn how to cook and do a lot of things an eighteen-year-old wouldn't normally need to know. He decided we'd all learn how to cook, and we would have these times when we tried out new recipes. I'll never forget Eddie mixing apple and beef in this casserole thing. It was gross, and I was maybe seven. I spat it straight out."

"Can I ask…? I mean…."

Ryan rescued him. "You want to know why did Saul have custody of us all at eighteen?"

"Yeah. You don't have to say if it's not something…. I mean, we all have secrets."

"It's no secret. You could google me if you want. This bar was originally my grandad's—my mom's dad, that is. She inherited it, married my dad, had Saul really young, then waited a while for the others, who she had close together. I was an accident, or so Saul tells me."

"A good one, I think," Jordan said when Ryan paused. Anything to banish this strange tone in Ryan's voice.

"Apparently so. Saul remembers our mom being pregnant and very happy. I was maybe six weeks old, and Dad decided Mom needed a night out, just the two of them, with Saul babysitting. He'd negotiated that against his eighteenth birthday celebration the week before. They allowed him the bar for it, albeit with soft drinks only, and he in turn covered for them to have a weekend away."

Jordan waited for the end to this story; it couldn't be good.

"They died that weekend," Ryan said. "A drive-by shooting, just bystanders waiting in line for a movie."

"Shit, I'm so sorry."

"It was so long ago now. They found the guys who did it. Drugs were involved, and my parents were two of six people shot. The cops came to us, and Saul just stepped up. He took on everything, put his plans for college on hold, ran the bar with a family friend who held the license for him until he was of legal age to have it. He brought up a baby and his three other brothers. Saul was the glue that kept us together."

"You're close."

"All of us, yes."

Jordan felt a lot of things: compassion, sadness, and an overwhelming need to touch Ryan. He covered Ryan's hand with his own. "Saul did a good job. I've only met you and Jason, but Jason is professional and respectful, and you're just…."

"Just?"

"You. Sexy, strong, and gorgeous."

Silence. Jordan watched for Ryan's mood to shift, but all he did was smile that soft smile of his.

"I have dessert," he said finally.

"You do?" Jordan patted his belly. "Not sure I can fit it in."

"Family recipe. You have to try it."

"What?"

"This chocolate cake with cherries and—"

"You had me at chocolate."

"We can take it up with us while I read the script."

Part of Jordan didn't want to move. He'd just eaten an entire meal with Ryan, and he didn't want it to end. But moving upstairs meant the sofa and the intriguing door leading to the bedroom.

Between them they cleared away the mess dinner had caused, and then Ryan decided Jordan was in charge of taking the wine and glasses up. Ryan would carry the cake, plates, and cutlery.

"Leave the cake for a while?" Ryan asked.

"God, yes." Jordan patted his belly again.

Ryan's gaze slipped south, before very quickly rising back to meet Jordan's. There was a flash of heat there, and then confusion, before he indicated the sofa and sat down.

Once there, Ryan pulled over his laptop and fired it up again. The script was still open. Jordan placed the wine bottle and his glass on the coffee table and curled up in the opposite corner, sipping the red wine and watching Ryan's expression.

"What does the thing in brackets mean?" Ryan asked.

"Parentheticals indicate action or attitude direction for a character. So if it says, I don't know, something like 'over phone,' it means the character is reacting as if they're receiving a phone call. The way you might stand when you're listening to someone, the things you might do, that kind of direction."

"Okay."

Ryan went back to reading, the only sound his steady breathing and the tap of his finger on the mousepad to scroll down. From this position, Jordan got free rein to stare. Ryan's profile was just as sexy as seeing him face to face.

Which of course got him thinking about Ryan naked because that was exactly how his brain was working right now.

And that wasn't a good idea.

So, he sipped more wine and considered what to do with himself while he waited. He pulled out his cell phone, but even the visual evidence of emails waiting didn't have him opening it to check. He placed it on the table next to the wine and instead leaned back into the cushions and relaxed.

This was nice, this downtime. The first he'd had in a long time.

He closed his eyes and centered his thoughts, pushing back the embarrassment and slight anxiety about someone reading his script.

"Hang on." Ryan's voice sounded loud in the otherwise quiet room.

Jordan opened his eyes and saw Ryan looking right at him. "What?"

"This is a gay romance. Two men. Together. Christmas."

"Yeah." Jordan dipped his gaze, unaccountably shy and not knowing what to say.

"The network would show this?"

Jordan shrugged, but spoke with conviction, from the heart. This was his project, his baby. "I'm going to work on it, start sowing the seed, maybe five years down the line. I don't know. I'd just like something for the guys out there who think there isn't romance for us, to show them there's magic in romance and Christmas for everyone."

"Shit," Ryan groaned, low in his throat.

"What? Is it bad?"

Ryan shook his head, but he closed the computer and very carefully placed it on the table. "You can't say things like that, with all that feeling and purpose."

"Sorry?" Jordan was alarmed. Ryan looked all tense, as if Jordan had just done something very wrong.

And then Ryan moved.

Smoothly he took the glass from Jordan, put it down, and kind of loomed over him. Then with a soft curse, he kissed Jordan with absolute purpose, tongue tracing the seam of Jordan's lips until he opened his mouth and took as much as he could.

All too soon the kisses were deep and somehow—*God knows how*—they were lying awkwardly side by side on the sofa, and Ryan had his hands on Jordan's ass, and he scooped him around until Jordan lay sprawled on top of him.

"We doing this?" Ryan asked.

"Yes," Jordan managed.

"You're so fucking sexy," Ryan added.

And to add emphasis to that, he bent his knees up and rolled his hips so they aligned better, all the time kissing Jordan. Ryan moved his hands along Jordan's back and traced them up and under his shirt; his touch was firm, pressing Jordan down and against him until Jordan couldn't move.

He didn't want to move.

Instead he lost himself in the kiss, stretched out like a cat in the sunshine over the wide expanse of Ryan's chest, against the length of him, lost in thoughts of getting his hands on Ryan's skin.

He'd not done this before, just kissing. Well, more than kissing; he was learning the taste of his lover and knowing it like his own.

Ryan pulled at Jordan's shirt, and between them they removed it, although for a second Jordan thought it would all end horribly when the collar caught behind his ear. Ryan chuckled as he eased it around. With another push from his strong thighs, Jordan was higher up, and Ryan pushed a hand between them and brushed across Jordan's nipples, hardwired to his cock. Jordan moaned into the kisses, and pressed his hands to the sofa, supporting his weight and shifting a little so he was looming over Ryan.

He really hoped Ryan got the message.

And thank God, he did. Ryan pinched each nipple in turn, playing with them, and then, at an extremely awkward angle, he sucked on each one as Jordan wriggled against him.

Jordan wanted more, and Ryan apparently knew; he sucked a mark right close to one, then used his teeth, tugging, and twisting with his fingers, and Jordan felt like he could come from that alone.

"You like that?" Ryan asked, his tone serious. "You want harder?"

Jordan let out a noise he'd never heard himself make before, a cross between a yes and a groan, and Ryan went to work, pulling harder and rolling his hips, and jeez…

He was going to come in his underwear, just from freaking nipple play. "We need to… need… bed," he managed and even tried to lever himself up, but Ryan was having none of it.

"Stay still," he ordered, his tone firm.

And God, that voice. Jordan pressed down, and then Ryan's hands were *right there* on his button, cleverly slipping it open, then the fly, and then—Fuck—his hand was closing around Jordan's cock and the noise Jordan made at the touch was just plain embarrassing: half plea, half warning. He lost himself in the sensation, arching his back a little. He didn't need to move; Ryan's height meant he could suck on Jordan's nipples and give him the best hand job of his entire *freaking* life.

"Close," Jordan groaned. "Ryan…."

"Come on, then," Ryan murmured against his chest. "Let me see it."

Jordan arched over, looked right down into Ryan's dark eyes, and lost himself in their depths. Then he was coming hard all over Ryan's hand in a wash of heat, and he couldn't help his curse at completion. For a second or more, he was unfocused, moving erratically through each pump against Ryan, and then he was spent. But he didn't collapse onto Ryan; he wanted to make Ryan come as hard.

"What do you want?" he asked, his voice husky, his head buzzing with the high of orgasm.

"Suck me," Ryan said, his tone brooking no argument.

Jordan was embarrassingly fast as he scrambled to get his hand on Ryan's cock, slipping off the length of his lover's body and falling to his knees next to him on the floor. The floor was hard, but he wasn't about to stop. He had Ryan's jeans open and shoved down low enough to get his first real look.

Gorgeous—the weight of him, the size, the flared head, and Jordan almost licked his lips. He was good at this, knew every trick in the book, and he would have Ryan squirming and shouting his name in a second.

"Slowly," Ryan warned.

What? Slowly? "What if I want to go fast?"

Ryan looked at him, raising an eyebrow as if to say, "Do what I tell you."

Fuck, that's hot.

So, he set to work with his tongue and hands, loving every sound Ryan made. He leaned up and over Ryan, swallowing as much of the length as he could, but something was missing…. Then he realized what it was. Without looking, he located one of Ryan's hands and tugged at it to rest it on his head, pressing it hard so that Ryan got the idea.

The cock in his mouth jumped as Ryan twisted his hand into Jordan's hair and held him still.

"You want me to fuck your mouth?" Ryan's voice was nothing more than a rasp now.

Jordan made a noise around the mouthful of cock, a groan of assent, and then he held still, allowing Ryan to press deeper; and then Ryan pulled out.

"Fuck," Ryan groaned, "your mouth."

They set up a rhythm, and the prickle of sensation as Ryan gripped his hair had Jordan reaching for his own cock, which was making a valiant attempt at getting back in the game.

"Close…," Ryan rasped.

Then it was Ryan's turn, and he released his hold on Jordan's hair.

He was trying to pull away. "No," Jordan grumbled around Ryan's cock.

Ryan's hand returned after a moment, twisting again and finding an anchor. "Oh fuck, Jordan…"

His pushing became more erratic, and Jordan sucked as hard as he could, using his tongue, the brush of his teeth, anything to get Ryan over the edge.

"Fuck!" Ryan shouted.

And he was coming, the heat of him down Jordan's throat: one pulse, two, releasing the hold on Jordan's hair and the last of his spend smearing at the corner of Jordan's mouth.

"Jesus," Ryan muttered. And then somehow he manhandled Jordan up and over him so they could kiss again.

The kisses were lazy, erotic slides of tongues and an exchange of air, until finally Ryan cradled Jordan's face and looked up at him in all seriousness.

"What do you see in a small-town sheriff?" he asked with his dark gaze fixed firmly to Jordan's.

"Easy," Jordan murmured. "You're sex on legs, you're firm and determined, you smile a lot. And fuck, your cock is a thing of beauty."

Clearly he said the right thing somewhere in all of that because Ryan chuckled and hugged him close.

"Good answer," he said.

CHAPTER 10

~ *Adam* ~

Adam moved some bowls, picked them up, put them down and in general fussed around like he was expecting a visit from strangers who would care what the place looked like.

Ethan read his actions. "It's just Justin and Sam," he reassured him and took the bowls from Adam's hands and placed them on the table.

"I can't help it." Adam did a three–sixty, checking out their place. It never failed to make him smile that he and Ethan had this place and were together. Well, he'd smile normally. Tonight he couldn't smile, couldn't even summon up the pretense of a smile. The dreams wouldn't stop, and the dread in the pit of his stomach was enough to have him on edge.

Inviting Justin and Sam over for drinks and cards had been Ethan's idea. Something along the lines that the four of them needed normal.

Adam felt anything but normal. He felt scratchy and scared and a hundred other things he couldn't get ahold of and deal with. So he picked up the bowls, and Ethan cursed under his breath, took the bowls from him again, placed them on the counter, then pulled Adam close, pressing him to the wall by the door and holding him in place. For a second, Adam wriggled to move away, but Ethan was clearly in one of his "holding Adam still for his own good" moods.

"Adam, breathe."

"I'm fine," Adam snapped, then realized he actually wasn't breathing well at all. Fuck if the panic wasn't fluttering inside him and becoming something so big he couldn't stop it—

"Breathe for me, Adam."

So Adam tried. He inhaled the scent of his lover, his fiancé, and inhaled long and deep, letting the breath out gently, controlled. And all the time he twisted his hands into the material of Ethan's shirt, and Ethan just said over and over, "You're okay... I got you."

One day everything wouldn't be okay and Ethan would see right through him and be gone. How much longer would Ethan be able to put up with Adam and these stupid panic attacks and the blank slate where he should have memories?

Adam moved a little against the wall, the hardness at his back allowing him to straighten from a slumped mess. "Last night I saw it again."

"I guessed that." Ethan pressed a hand to Adam's chin, tilting his head so that Adam was looking at him. "You had a rough night."

"I'm sorry." The sorry was Adam's default answer to everything people said to him.

You look tired.

"I'm sorry."

We can cancel the next booking if you don't feel so good.

"I'm sorry."

You cried in your sleep.

"I'm so fucking sorry."

"Don't be sorry," Ethan said, his tone relaxed. "Nothing to be sorry about. Okay? Tonight will be good, normal. And if you need to talk to Justin, he'll be right there."

Adam shoved Ethan away, catching him by surprise so he tripped and ended up smacking against the far wall. Guilt churned with temper. "You arranged this so I'd talk to Justin?"

"No, sweetheart, I didn't. I just thought it would be a nice relaxed night with them."

Ethan's look of surprise had melted to something like compassion as he spoke.

Meanwhile the guilt in Adam grew and grew until it became a real thing eating away at his balance. "I pushed you," he said, horror in his voice.

Ethan stepped closer, placing the flat of his hand on Adam's chest and shoving him just as hard. Only he didn't have as far to go, and he flailed as he tried to catch himself as the wall met his back. Then Ethan was there, pushing a thigh between his legs and pressing hard, catching Adam's hands and sliding them up the wall so that he couldn't move.

"I can take anything you give me," Ethan said, in the dirtiest, sexiest, rawest voice, which had every knot of tension unraveling inside Adam.

The kiss was just as dirty—fierce, a clash of teeth and domination that had Adam hard and rubbing against Ethan, desperate for something, anything, to get him out of his own head.

A loud knock on the door. Ethan pulled away from the kiss and Adam wanted the visitors to go. He'd been so close to forgetting everything, and the last thing he wanted was to see anyone else.

"Ready?" Ethan asked. He was straightening his shirt, then pressing fingers to his lips. "Later, right?"

"Open up!" Sam shouted from outside. "Fucking cold."

Adam straightened his own clothes and nodded. "Ready."

He opened the door, and Sam tumbled in as if he'd been leaning on the door. Adam caught him at the same time as Ethan, and between the two of them, they stopped Sam face-planting and also caught the containers he was holding.

"Tell me you brought chilli." Ethan opened the corner of the first container, letting out a sigh of contentment at the scent inside. "Shut the door, little brother."

Justin pulled the door shut behind them, and Adam didn't know what to say.

They looked at each other for a second. At least that was okay, and Adam was able to look Justin in the eye.

"We need to clear the air," Justin said.

"Now?" This from Sam, who looked from Justin to Adam and back again. "Don't you want to eat first?"

Sam sounded concerned, and all Adam could think was that whatever they were going to talk about was going to be a fucking awful thing.

But suddenly he didn't want to be the only one with all of this in his head.

"When I dream, you're always there," Adam blurted out. "Tell me you weren't there, Justin. Tell me that you didn't kill those two men at the ranch who were protecting me or the guy who did my tattoo. *Tell me!*"

Ethan moved then, placing himself right between but to one side of his brother and his lover. "Guys—"

"I *was* there. At the ranch anyway."

"He should remember on his own," Ethan said a little desperately.

"Not when he's recalling things that aren't true." Justin's tone was flat and didn't hold any accusation.

Still, Adam winced at what he said, because, hell, how could he know whether what he was recalling was true or not?

"He'll work through it," Ethan said. "One memory at a time."

"I need to tell him." Justin was adamant.

"No, you don't. This isn't about you." Ethan stepped forward, and the last thing Adam wanted was for the two brothers to fight.

"We need to look at this like adults," Justin snapped, and he too moved forward a little, restrained anger in every inch of him.

"Tell me what you want to tell me," Adam said before Ethan and Justin came to blows.

"No," Ethan said.

Adam yanked him back with a forceful tug, and Ethan had no choice but to park his ass back to the counter with Adam.

"They said you should remember on your own," Ethan pointed out, his desperation turning to fear. He turned to Adam and cradled his face. "He could tell you anything and you wouldn't know any different."

Sam cursed. "*He* has a name and *he* wouldn't lie."

Jesus, now Sam was getting all defensive of Justin. This wasn't going the way Adam wanted it to go at all.

"Sam, don't." Justin stopped Sam from saying anything else. "Ethan is right. *My brother* knows how I could fuck with Adam if I wanted to, how I could twist this."

The emphasis on *brother* had Ethan wincing, but he still didn't take his eyes off Adam.

"Justin is a good man," Sam snapped.

Was this what it had come down to? Was Adam coming between the brothers with his stupid, fucking brain and memories? "It will be okay," he reassured Ethan. "You know your brother."

"That's not true. I don't know this new Justin at all," Ethan said.

Justin let out a soft noise of pain, and Adam had to stop this right now. Ethan loved his brother, and he certainly wouldn't say that normally. He was 100 percent behind Justin, swearing that he was a good man.

"I want to know," Adam insisted. "I don't want to make up memories in my head. Or have Justin think I'm scared of him or that I hate him."

Justin sighed heavily. "It's okay to hate me. I can handle it. I don't need anyone, and I'm a big boy."

"He doesn't hate you," Sam reassured. "And he needs me," he added softly.

Justin murmured something to Sam that sounded like an apology, and they held hands.

"Adam doesn't hate you," Ethan said. "I'm sorry, Justin. I didn't mean to say…"

Silence.

And then Justin snapped. "Adam should hate me!"

Sam's turn to move. The shortest and slightest of them, but it didn't mean no-one listened to him. "Table," he ordered. "Let's sit."

Numb, Adam took the nearest chair, with Justin opposite and Ethan next to him. Ethan took Adam's hand under the table and held tight. A touch of reassurance and enough to ground Adam.

"I was there, at the ranch. You're right to remember that," Justin began. He laid his hands on the table, and Sam reached over and took one of them in his.

Objectively, Adam saw the touch, knew that Justin had Sam's complete support, respect, and love. Sam knew Justin's heart, and knowing that made something unravel inside him. He needed to trust that he could know what was in Justin's heart too. He just had to accept there was a reason for Justin to be in the places he dreamed of, like the ranch and the tattoo shop.

Adam cleared his throat. "Did you…?"

Kill them?

"You know I killed people," Justin said, his eyes dark with emotion. "Does it matter if these were two on the list?"

"Fuck," Sam cursed. "Justin, we talked about this. Don't ramp up the fucking drama. Just tell Adam without all the dramatics."

Justin looked a little chastened and cast Sam a quick look of apology. "No, I didn't kill them," he admitted. "I was sent there for someone else." He focused right in on Adam. "You."

"Okay," Adam said evenly as Ethan squeezed his hand. "Not me though, right? You didn't know it was me. You just had a name. Right?"

"I didn't have anything but a name," Justin murmured. "The men there were already dead, I checked. And then I looked for my actual target—you—but you weren't there.

You'd gone. So, I don't know how you can see me killing them, because I didn't, and you weren't even there. It's just your mind playing tricks."

Adam closed his eyes and recalled the memory, or dream, or whatever the hell it was. "You were crouching over them," he said. "Or someone was."

"Are you just filling spaces with me?" Justin asked after a small pause. He didn't sound hurt or angry or shocked, or any of the emotions that Adam thought might follow. "When your memories return like they do, are you assuming I was there?"

"I don't know," Adam didn't open his eyes. "I don't know how this works. I thought you were dead," he said for the hundredth time since coming home.

"If I'd known you were there, if they'd ever told me... I would have come for you."

Justin's voice broke, and he opened his eyes to see Adam's bright with emotion. Abruptly it wasn't Adam who needed reassurance—it was Justin.

Adam reached over and pressed a hand over Justin's. Yes, he knew that was true. He truly believed that Justin would have moved heaven and earth for his best friend.

Now if only Adam could remember more so that all of this made sense in his head. Then he could reconcile Justin the friend who did things because he didn't know any better and because part of him had died, with Justin the killer in Adam's dreams.

That was on Adam.

"I need to focus harder."

"If you have questions?" Justin asked softly.

Adam shook his head. If he had to take it that Justin wasn't there, that maybe he was making things up along with recalling events, then he needed time to process this.

"Can we just try for a regular night?" Adam asked.

The rest of the evening passed quickly. They ate, and it wasn't entirely normal. There was an air of brittle tension that left Adam exhausted. Sam beat everyone at poker despite having the worst poker face. Adam suspected Justin was deliberately losing to his boyfriend just to keep the wild, childlike grin on Sam's face. They all needed Sam here tonight, settling them, centering their group, being the bridge between Adam and Justin.

Adam's mind wasn't fully on the game, but somehow they managed a kind of normality, as normal as this misfit group of four men could be.

After they left and it was just him and Ethan, all Adam wanted was to hug and then sleep.

"I love you," Ethan said into their kiss as they clambered onto the bed. "You were so brave tonight."

"I'm not brave."

Ethan huffed and did a flip maneuver that had him lying on top of Adam, pinning him to the mattress. Ethan was hard and ready, with focus in his eyes.

"Shut up, Adam," he ordered and then proceeded to make sure that Adam's mouth was way too busy to do any talking. And that his body was too exhausted for him to protest that he wanted to talk.

The dreams came again for Adam as he slept, but they changed a little. Tonight, Adam remembered visiting Justin at Crooked Tree as a grown man, even though this wasn't true.

Justin, as Adam knew him now, was also there in his dream crouching over bodies that laid in rows outside Branches, and then he stood and looked around himself. Suddenly he was back on the ranch where he'd been hidden in WITSEC.

And as he watched from wherever the hell he was standing, he saw Justin there, poking at dead bodies and then walking away holstering a gun.

When he woke up, sweating and desperate to get out of bed, he was disoriented and crying. Ethan rolled over in his sleep, pulling him close, not even waking up but gripping him hard. As if he knew Adam needed him.

If I am remembering the right things, then why didn't Justin see me there?

I wouldn't have known who he was, but why didn't Justin see me, and why didn't he save me?

CHAPTER 11

~ *Ryan* ~

The call came in at a little after 10:00 a.m., just after Ryan finished the last of his coffee. Someone had found a car abandoned on the side of the road, the doors open and no one in sight.

"Registration?"

"Andrew James Vale, thirty-seven, address in Missoula. No record of the car being reported stolen."

"Track down the owner."

"On it."

His deputy, Stefan, was brand new to the office, only a few days out of training, with good instincts but with a tendency to play everything by the rules—to the absolute letter of them, actually. He hadn't got to the point where he could make decisions for himself but that was okay with Ryan. Stefan seemed like a good guy, genial and easy to have around the office. Also, he made awesome coffee.

Stefan looked excited to have this action early on a Monday morning, and Ryan attempted to focus while actually feeling a small adrenaline rush at having something to do. He always left Mondays clear for admin, with no school visits or community action work, and it wasn't as if Jedburgh was a hotbed of drama. A stolen car was as good as it was going to get this early in the week.

Well, apart from Justin and Adam going missing all those years ago, but other than that....

They made good time. There had been no more snowfall over the weekend and the roads were clear and ice free.

The man hovering by the potentially stolen car visibly vibrated with excitement. "I stayed to help you, to make sure no one took it."

"We've got this now, sir," Stefan said. "Thank you."

The man pressed ahead. "My name is Oscar Dryden. Do you need to write that down? It's just that I don't often see someone pulled over up here, and I'd have missed it if the snow hadn't melted off some, and then I looked inside and it was empty, and there is a kid's car seat in the back, and so I got to thinking that—"

"Sir," Stefan interrupted, "I have your name. If you could give us a number, we'll contact you if we need anything else."

Oscar read out his cell number; Stefan made a note of it, took some other details and then photos, while Ryan considered what he had in front of him. He waited for Stefan to report on what he'd found as soon as Oscar drove away. Ryan recognized the man from town, one of the new home owners who worked in Missoula and lived out here in lower-cost housing, commuting to the city every day. When he left, they began to sort things out.

"Okay, one empty and abandoned car," Ryan said. "What did you find on the owner?"

"Andrew James Vale, thirty-seven. Wife Pauline Marie, twenty-nine, and son Simon, six. No report of a stolen car. I've put a call in with the local cops to do a house visit."

Ryan leaned into the car, careful not to touch anything. "Tell me what you see," he said.

Stefan straightened his shoulders, looking every inch the newbie. "Mazda, maybe five or six years old, good condition," He touched the bonnet. "Cold. Car is tidy inside, kiddie seat explained by young son. Hmmm."

"What? What is it you see?"

Stefan leaned into the car and pulled out a juice cup, a giraffe plushie, and a child's coat. He considered each item before turning his attention to the front of the car, then pulled on latex gloves and checked the glovebox, bringing out some documents.

They both heard the sound of a cell phone at the same time.

Stefan located it and pulled the cell from where it had slipped down beside a seat. He frowned at the display and answered the phone on speaker.

"Mr. Vale?"

Ryan answered, "No, this is Sheriff Carter, Jedburgh, Montana."

"This is Missoula PD calling the number we have for Mr. Andrew Vale."

"I have the phone, it was in his car. We're following a lead that he has gone into the woods from here. Can you connect to dispatch." Ryan gave the PD the number for his office so they could go through the correct protocols to establish who Ryan was and to form a connection between the two departments.

"Will do, Sheriff."

The call ended and Stefan looked up at Ryan. "This man could have just left the cell in the car before it was stolen."

"One possibility," Ryan agreed.

He expanded his search around the car. The snow was hard-packed there, mixed in with mud, and he crouched to look at footprints messed up with their own and likely Dryden's, the guy who found the car.

Stefan joined him. "Could be that whoever drove the car went into the woods."

"This is Crooked Tree land, but the very edge of it. We're miles away from any places to hide," Ryan said absently. This road was the eastern edge of the ranch.

Stefan's radio crackled, and Ryan listened in as he circled the car.

The words over the airwaves cut right through Ryan and Stefan.

"Attending Missoula cops located the wife. She's been badly beaten, is unconscious, and has been removed to the hospital. No sign of husband and child on the property."

The summary was clear and concise, but Ryan heard the wavering in the dispatcher's voice...

"Neighbors reported an altercation. Missoula PD is putting out an Amber Alert. God." Dispatch went quiet, and then Ryan heard the clearing of a throat. "Andrew Vale is to be considered armed and potentially dangerous. Do you copy that, Sheriff?"

"Copy. Call for backup to this location," he ordered.

He'd heard enough. He drew his weapon and Stefan copied, his eyes narrowed. Should they wait? There was a potentially armed man out there with his kid. Was he intending to hurt the boy? Or was this something else? Ryan had to go with his gut feeling, and he exchanged nods with Stefan. They were going after the man with the gun.

The two officers picked their way through piled snow and into the woods beyond, spotting blood about ten feet in and more scarlet fifteen feet farther on. They found the father soon after that. At least, that was who Ryan imagined it must be. He'd taken his own life with a gun shot to his face, which was now mangled and open. If the dad had been bleeding before he shot himself, then Ryan couldn't see any obvious evidence of it, which could mean one awful thing: the kid was there, and he was hurt.

"Christ," Stefan said and gagged.

Ryan couldn't react, he had to be the experienced one, yet he couldn't bring himself to look at the dead man. *Don't let me find the boy dead. Please let him still be alive.*

He gestured for Stefan to wait.

"Simon?" Ryan called out. "Are you here? I'm a sheriff. Police," he expanded. "Simon?"

Nothing. No noise at all.

He tried again. "Simon? Are you hurt? Simon?" Then he listened carefully over the forest silence. The snow muffled his voice, and there was nothing else here. No birds, only the odd sound of snow falling from a tree, or ice crackling on branches. "Simon! Call out!"

He shouted and waited, shouted and waited. And then he heard it, a soft whimper, a cry, and he held up a hand to Stefan. "Call this in. Get the coroner and paramedics here." Then he headed immediately in the direction of the sound, as well as he could judge it.

Stumbling and forging through piles of snow and onto flat ground sheltered by trees and fallen trunks, he didn't have to go far. "Simon? I'm here to help you."

"Mommy" was all he heard.

And then he saw the kid—a slight boy with bright red hair and so much blood on his face. His lip was split and he had a cut over his eye that explained all the blood. He was cowering, dressed in just a sweatshirt, and his skin was white-blue with cold.

Ryan immediately crouched next to him, shrugging off his coat and reaching out. Whether it was the uniform or the fact that little Simon was in shock, he didn't know, but the boy crawled the short distance in the snow and came straight to the coat. Ryan wrapped him tight and pulled the hood up, and like that, he carried him to his car, taking the long way around the body of Simon's father. They might have a long wait for the nearest paramedic, and God, he hoped it was Aaron on duty.

At first he tried to set Simon on the passenger seat, but the boy was having none of it and gripped him tightly. So holding Simon close, Ryan settled them both into the seat. He sat there with the heater on, Simon wrapped in his coat, and waited. When the ambulance arrived, Ryan was never happier to see Aaron, who efficiently assessed Simon, with the child gripping Ryan's hand throughout.

"This is my brother, Aaron," Ryan explained. Simon was listening to him. "And his partner, Lucy. They'll look after you."

"I want my mommy," Simon whimpered.

"We'll find her, buddy." Ryan nodded at Aaron over Simon's head. "She's in Missoula." He left that hanging and waited for Aaron to respond, knowing his brother understood.

"We'll take you straight to her," Aaron said.

"We will?" Lucy asked, looking between the brothers.

Ryan looked at her with his best pleading expression. "Please?"

"This is our last call, so we're off the clock now," Lucy said. "Let's go straight to Missoula and find your mommy."

Those words and Lucy's kind manner encouraged Simon to go with her.

"I'll text you the details of where she is," Ryan said and watched the ambulance leave and the coroner arrive.

He recalled the terror on Simon's expression and wished that today had been just another quiet Monday.

Ryan didn't really need an excuse to visit Crooked Tree, but he wanted to report what had happened on their land. And also, more importantly in a personal way, he really wanted to see Jordan. Because really, when it came down to it, he needed a hug at least, a chance to connect to normal. What happened today was the first of its kind for Ryan: a child being witness to so much trauma and Ryan being in the middle of it.

The last time he'd dealt with anything that raw had been to break the news to a family that their daughter had overdosed at college. The pain was real, and naked, and even though he stayed professional on the outside, inside he was dying a little bit.

He had this crazy idea that a hug from Jordan, or a touch, or hell, just a smile, might make his day better.

But they'd have to get past the awkwardness of their night together.

Not the sex, that had been hot and vital and needed. It was the way they'd had sex that worried Ryan, because yet again he'd let out his stubborn-in-charge persona and probably scared Jordan away.

Jordan had left early that night, after some half-assed, awkward conversation about how good the sex was, and with Ryan on the high of mutual orgasms and some really intense kissing, saying they should really do it again.

Who the hell says that? Way to come off as needy and pathetic.

But it wasn't as if Jordan said anything to stop Ryan talking, and Ryan had hated the silence, so he filled it talking about how he wanted more.

The awkward that happened after was all on Jordan. Ryan had lost his head on that sofa, gotten all toppy and pushy, and Jordan had left. Also—and sue him for his idiot brain—but Ryan still couldn't understand outside of his confident-in-bed personality, what the hell did pretty, sparkly, happy Jordan see in him?

And yes, he knew damn well he was being freaking irrational. But the last words they'd spoken had been a stupid exchange about how Ryan had muscles and was tall but how the cake he ate made him soft in the middle, and how much Jordan loved that slight vulnerability in such a strong, sexy man.

Jordan had said that while laying his head on said belly, much as Jake and Milly did; it was reminiscent of how his brothers poked at him. Ryan wasn't carrying much weight, but he wasn't toned and ripped like Aaron was, nor slim, and cute like his nearest-in-age brother, Jason.

Insecurity was a bitch, something that he didn't normally carry into sex, but hell, on the morning after—or in this case the hour after? Yeah, insecurity hit him like a Mack truck.

Jordan had sent him a text later that day, a thank you in a somewhat confused message that suggested Ryan call him so they could do it again.

Ryan didn't call.

Jordan didn't call.

Three days and no call later…

Three days Ryan had left it without contacting Jordan in reply.

There hadn't been any more texts.

The ball was in his court, and he'd fucked it up big time.

Then today had happened: the father killing himself, the son traumatized but still with his mother, and abruptly seeing Jordan was all Ryan wanted to do. He got to the ranch, reported the incident on the edge of Crooked Tree land to Jay, kept it to a minimum of information; Jay shook his hand, compassion in his eyes. Jay was like that, all supportive and understanding, and Ryan didn't need that or he might snap. So, he left quickly with a goodbye, and he didn't look back.

Was this what it was like to find someone who wormed their way into your soul? Was this what Jay had with Nate? This scratching, clawing need to be with someone.

I'm losing it. I barely know the man.

Just as he was pulling up down by the Forest Cabins where the film crew were, he took a phone call from Aaron. "Hey, how's it going at the hospital?"

"The mom's awake, and the kid is with her. She's holding it together for Simon, but she said that her husband hadn't been the same since he'd been let go by his company last winter. She wouldn't look at me when she spoke, though, as if she was done with it all and just wanted to hold Simon. Jeez, it was intense."

"Did Simon say anything to you on the way there?"

"He spoke a little to me. Said his dad promised him McDonald's, only he didn't stop driving and it scared him. According to Simon, he asked his dad to stop so he could have a pee, and he ran over to the trees. Sketchy details, but apparently he fell. His father picked him up, saw the blood, and was crying, and he told Simon he was sorry and he should run before he hurt him. I think the kid was confused and scared—Jesus, he was terrified, actually."

"So, the father didn't mean to hurt his son?"

"I'm not the cop here, but I don't think his dad was thinking of anything at all."

"Shit. Poor kid." *Poor family.*

"Simon heard the shot and stayed right where he was. He said he couldn't move because his dad had told him he had to stay away from him."

"Is he okay?"

Aaron paused. He was the most thoughtful of Ryan's brothers, the one who could see a situation and sum it up very quickly. But this seemed to be stumping him.

"The kid's not doing so well," he began with caution, "but he's in the best place, with his mom."

"Thanks for taking Simon all the way there."

"No worries."

"I owe you one."

There was silence and Ryan knew that both he and Aaron were in the throes of processing what had happened. Between him, Aaron and Jason, they shared a lot of first responder experiences and sometimes they needed to think about them apart.

Today, hearing Aaron's voice was a day that Ryan needed to share this with a brother.

"You still owe me loads." Aaron chuckled and broke the silence.

Ryan could go with this. He could play pretend for a few seconds of normality, and the ritual teasing was normal, a gallows humor. "Like what?"

"From that one time I kept your big gay secret," Aaron teased.

This was a standing joke. Aaron had found a stash of porn under Ryan's bed when Ryan was just short of fourteen, tickled the admission of gayness out of him, and then vowed not to tell a soul… until Jason came in from school and then every freaking Carter brother had to know. Not a single one of them threw him out or seemed disgusted, though. Jason had helpfully pointed out that statistically one gay brother out of five was about the going rate.

To this day, Ryan didn't know if Jason had been fucking with all of them. "You kept the secret for an hour before telling everyone," he pointed out.

"Better out than in," Aaron added.

"Ha-freaking-ha," Ryan said without heat and ended his call to Aaron.

Then he sat in the car awhile, calling Stefan with the update and thinking about the day. He'd seen things like that before—parents back from war, parents caught up in financial messes where the only way out was to take their own lives. Seeing it before didn't make little Simon's story any easier. He didn't have a dad now.

This is stupid, he thought, *I need to go before I do something stupid.*

A knock on his window startled him and he pushed open the door. Angie stood there with her ever-present clipboard.

"Sheriff? Is everything okay?" She glanced down at her notes. "Did we have a meeting? I don't have anything on my schedule. We're just wrapping up for today. Loss of light." She held up a hand and then pressed it to her ear. "No, I said we needed the whole scene. I think it would be more effective."

He opened his mouth to ask what she meant, then realized she was talking into a phone, or something a lot more efficient, considering this area of the ranch was something of a dead spot for cell reception.

"Jesus, Artie, do I have to come over there—okay, on my way." She looked at Ryan. "Sorry, I have to go. So, we didn't have an appointment?"

"No. I was just hoping to see Jordan."

She didn't seem to think that was a weird thing. In fact, she smiled widely.

"Jordan is in the blue tent checking scripts for tomorrow. We were on exteriors today, very cold." Then she winked, and Ryan was startled a little as she added, "He probably needs warming up."

She vanished at great speed up the hill toward a green tent, while Ryan locked his car and zipped up his jacket. All he could fixate on was the concept of Jordan needing warming up.

Ryan found him in the huge blue tent with the sign proclaiming this was Production HQ. Jordan was bent over a table, looking down at sheets of paper laid out in front of him, talking to Micah.

Ryan took a moment to look at the man he'd had writhing in his arms only a few days ago. He was so like Micah, yet at the same time so different. Ryan had looked at the publicity stills for the show they'd been in as teens, and while they were definitely twins, there were differences. Jordan had a slightly thinner face and his eyes were darker, but it wasn't just that. There was a tension in him; he held himself very stiffly at times, as if he had the weight of the world on his shoulders, whereas Micah seemed a whole lot more relaxed. Then there was the way they spoke.

Micah looked up and saw Ryan, smiled at him, and offered a "Yo, Sheriff."

Ryan wasn't sure it was appropriate for him to yo back, so he sketched a wave and added a soft "Hello."

Jordan also looked up, seeming a little startled to see Ryan there. He straightened and gave a half-smile. "Hey," he offered. "Is everything okay? Were we scheduled for a meeting?"

Ryan wanted to be honest, but Micah was standing right the hell there.

As if Micah sensed it—or maybe because Ryan was standing there looking like a complete idiot—he picked up a couple of sheets of paper and made his way out of the tent.

"Later, J," he said to Jordan and clapped Ryan on the shoulder as he left. "Cheer the fucker up," he muttered.

"I heard that!" Jordan shouted.

"You were supposed to!" Micah returned.

Ryan wasn't sure what to say. "Is everything okay?" he asked and waggled a finger to suggest the filming, or the crew, or the freaking tent, or God knows what.

"Yeah, mostly. Why are you here?"

Ryan sighed. This wasn't going well. "I had a bad day as well." He didn't expand, but it didn't look like he was getting a hug from Jordan right then, so he needed to leave and find a brother or two he could talk to.

"You didn't return the text," Jordan blurted out, interrupting Ryan's thoughts. "Shit, I wasn't going to say that. I was going to act all normal—because I can do that, I'm an actor. But seeing you, I just wanted to know what I did to fuck up, because I'm not used to anything but hooking up on the down-low, so I clearly did something way stupid."

"You didn't—"

"Is it because I'm not out properly and that you feel like I'm using you, or is it because you just don't like me? Or because I just laid there and let you take over? Should I have been more—" He waved his hand to indicate more of whatever *more* was.

Ryan's mouth fell open as he processed all of that. "*What?*" he finally managed when his brain caught up with what Jordan had said.

Jordan scrubbed his eyes with his fists. "Oh God," he said miserably. "It's because I said I really like you, and that's freaked you out, and I'm too fucking needy. That's it, isn't it?"

Ryan walked up to him and pulled Jordan's hands away from his face. In a smooth move, he had Jordan pressed up against one of the poles holding up the tent and was kissing him like they might never kiss again. At first Jordan wriggled to get away—that only lasted a few seconds—and then he was clasping his hands behind Ryan's neck and holding on for the ride. In turn, Ryan wrapped his arms around Jordan and the pole and held tight. There was no way Jordan was moving until he fully understood that Ryan didn't think he was too needy or that he'd fucked up somehow.

Jordan's hands slid up into Ryan's hair, twisting there and holding the kiss, and Ryan used his knee to part Jordan's thighs and slot himself there. He had to lift Jordan slightly because of the height difference, and Jordan moaned so loudly into the kiss that Ryan thought he'd hurt him, and he pulled away slightly.

"Are you okay?" he asked, his breathing heavy.

Jordan answered by grinding down on Ryan's thigh and leaning in to deepen the kiss.

"You're getting company."

Micah's voice interrupted the kissing and Ryan stumbled back and glanced over at the entrance to the tent. He saw Micah there with his back to Ryan and Jordan.

"Production team meeting," Micah added over his shoulder.

Ryan couldn't believe what he'd just done—nearly rubbed himself off against a man who wasn't out, in the middle of the day in front of who-the-fuck-ever could have walked in. "I'm sorry," he said and backed away again, ass hitting the table with the papers on top.

Jordan raised a hand to his lips, and then he smiled before deliberately rearranging himself and yanking down his thick fleece to cover the bulge in his jeans. "Don't be sorry. I'm guessing you're still interested."

"Have you seen yourself?" Ryan said. "Of course I'm interested. I'm sane and healthy, end of story."

Jordan tilted his head a little. "Then why didn't you text me back?"

Ryan pushed the insecurities down to where they normally stayed. "Because I am a sheriff in the middle of Montana, with a soft belly, and shit. I say again, have you seen yourself?"

"I love your soft bits," Jordan murmured. Then he winked again. "And your hard bits."

"They're coming over," Micah announced.

Ryan heard voices as whoever formed the production team headed their way. That was a good thing, because he didn't know how to process the teasing without some real forethought.

Jordan said quietly, "We should be finished by eight. I could be at your place by nine?"

Ryan took a step closer and half whispered, "Yes."

And then, before there was any chance of giving in to the temptation of Jordan's damp, well-kissed lips, Ryan left. He exchanged pleasantries with the people arriving and received a knowing glance from Angie, to which he replied with a quirk of his lips.

She and Micah knew, but they were safe people to know the man Jordan truly was. How much of a secret could this be for Jordan anyway? He must have so many people in the industry aware of who he really was. If there was any hope of this being more than just a couple of weeks of sex, then they needed to talk about it at some point.

Because Ryan really wanted to know more about Jordan Darby, and the lust he had for the sexy man was overwhelming.

Somehow along the way he'd forgotten about Simon and what he'd seen there, but it settled around him again when he reached his car.

He owed it to himself to make sure he talked to Jordan, that he didn't push what had happened today under the carpet. If Jordan wanted to be a part of his life, albeit for a couple of weeks, then maybe Ryan was better off telling him how he was feeling.

That he felt brittle and unsettled, and he really needed a hug.

CHAPTER 12

~ *Jordan* ~

Jordan stopped at the bar and exchanged pleasantries with Saul; at least, he spoke to the man as little as he could get away with. He wanted to be upstairs with Ryan, and he wanted that *now*.

He took the proffered beers—no wine this time—and then went through the door and straight up the stairs to Ryan's room. He raised his hand to knock, but the door flew open and Ryan near-dragged him in, yanking him past the door, shutting it, and then pushing him up against the wall.

He let out another one of those embarrassing whimpers; his cock was hard and he wrapped his hands around Ryan's neck, despite the bottle of beer in each. Nothing mattered at that moment. All he wanted was to come, to taste and climb and lose himself in Ryan.

The lust was madness, and it consumed him.

Ryan untangled his hands, took the beer from them, and placed them on the chair. He fell to his knees, all grace and sexy bedroom eyes.

"What are you...?" Jordan began, but stopped when it became way past obvious exactly what Ryan was doing.

In a smooth move, with no discussion or hesitation, Ryan had Jordan's jeans and underwear pulled down enough to be able to tug at Jordan's hard cock and then swallow him down.

There was no finesse, just desperate need, and all Jordan could do was scrabble uselessly at the wall and try to balance himself.

He wasn't going to last long, not with the noises Ryan was making around his cock, not with the absolute determination in Ryan's touch, the way he cursed when he couldn't get enough of Jordan and had to pull the material down farther.

Jordan had been on edge since earlier, when Ryan had nearly made him throw caution to the wind and rub himself off against Ryan's thigh.

Ryan stopped for a moment. "I've wanted to taste you so bad." He circled Jordan's cock with his hand and held it still for a second, then looked up at Jordan. "Gorgeous," he murmured.

Jordan had been on the receiving end of blow jobs before, but this was in a different league. Ryan was focused, unhurried, and his strength was the only thing keeping Jordan standing. Well, that and the wall behind him.

"Ryan," Jordan gasped and pushed forward into Ryan's mouth, biting out a rough curse of apology.

But Ryan didn't stop, and Jordan begged for more until he was so close he could taste the high of orgasm. Then Ryan stopped; he removed the delicious suction and instead stood and tugged Jordan away from the wall, pulling him toward that door at the back of the room.

Walking with his jeans around his thighs was awkward, and Jordan yanked Ryan to a stop. Ryan looked confused until Jordan toed off his sneakers and removed his jeans, and the heat in his gaze was so fucking sexy.

"Bed," Ryan said. "Now."

He didn't give Jordan a moment to stop, stealing another kiss and walking backward, guiding Jordan through the door. They didn't stop for Ryan to tell Jordan that this was the bedroom, or hell, indulge in any social niceties at all. They tumbled onto the bed, kissing, with Ryan shoving at his own clothes and then at Jordan's shirt until they were naked against each other on top of the covers.

They kissed and rutted, and Ryan made a lot of promises about how he was going to make Jordan come so hard he'd forget his own name. The talk, the grinding, Ryan's hand on his cock, and orgasm slammed into Jordan, an explosion of heat and lust.

And Jordan couldn't breathe, or speak, a boneless mess on the bed.

Ryan loomed over him, staring right down at him, such focus in his dark eyes as he slipped his hands up and down his own cock. He looked close, utterly focused on Jordan.

Jordan attempted to pull him closer, but Ryan wouldn't move, so Jordan concentrated on the parts he could reach, twisting and pulling on Ryan's nipples as he watched his expression, triumphant when it was Ryan's turn to lose it as he rutted into his hand, pressed against Jordan's belly.

Once done, he fell next to Jordan and they lay there for a few moments.

"Wow," Jordan began. "Hello to you too."

"Sorry." Ryan rolled up on one elbow to look down at him. "I should have said hello first."

Jordan wanted to wipe away the remorse on Ryan's face. "That was a hello, and a freaking great hello at that. It made my day better." Jordan flashed a quick grin. "We just lost two scenes because of shitty lighting."

"Is that bad?"

"It will cost us, but I think if we get back to it tomorrow, we could pull it back. You said you were having a bad day?"

"Oh, yeah." Ryan stopped and looked confused, as though he didn't know how to explain it.

"Do you want to talk about it?"

Ryan lay back on his pillow and crossed his hands behind his head. That way every muscle was prominent, and call him shallow, but all Jordan wanted to do was lick every glorious, muscled inch of him.

"A father on the edge committed suicide. He had his little boy with him." Ryan closed his eyes as if he couldn't bear to see Jordan's reaction.

"Is the boy okay?" Jordan had images of the father driving his car off a bridge or something and taking the child with him. Jesus, who did that kind of thing?

"He's with his mom."

Jordan let out a sigh of relief. "That's good, then."

Ryan still didn't open his eyes. "Far from good. The dad shot himself, with his son cowering in the snow not twenty feet away."

Compassion welled inside Jordan. "That poor kid." Then it hit him. Ryan's bad day was a hell of a lot worse than Jordan's. A bad day at Darby Films cost money, but a kid witnessing his dad's death? That wasn't a bad day, that was a nightmare.

He moved up and laid his head on Ryan's chest, tucking his hands underneath him and holding him tight. "Sorry," he said. Like that could maybe be enough.

Ryan let out a breath and then moved his hands to encourage Jordan to scoot higher until his head tucked under Ryan's chin. They lay there for a long time holding each other.

"This is what I needed," Ryan murmured.

Jordan pressed a soft kiss to the nearest inch of skin, a soft punctuation to the sadness in Ryan.

Ryan sighed. "I had this whole speech…."

"About what?"

"…For when you arrived here. About how I know you're only in town for a few weeks, but I can be your secret for as long as you need me, no strings attached, because I really want you in my bed. And God, I needed a hug, but when I saw you… I lost it."

That should be the best thing Jordan had heard—but it wasn't. He was confused, so he said nothing. Which, of course, was the wrong thing to do. Typically, he'd fucked up.

"Or not." Ryan's tone was suddenly flat. "We can just call it quits now."

In a flurry of movement, Jordan rose up and pinned him to the bed. "No, that's the wrong direction," he began, then realized he was making absolutely no sense. "I don't want to have limits on how long this lasts, Ryan. I'd like to think we could get to know each other better, because this is different to a hook-up."

Ryan blinked up at him. "It is?"

Shit, so Jordan had misread the situation again. Maybe Ryan just wanted the time Jordan was here and wasn't interested in anything else. "It doesn't have to be," he said. "If you don't want it to—"

The words were cut off by Ryan kissing him and wrestling him onto his back. "Stop talking. We both need to stop talking," he announced. "I like you, you like me. Let's just have sex and worry about the other parts later."

"Are you okay, though? Do you need to talk? I can listen if you need me." *I want to be needed.*

Ryan nodded, his troubled gaze clearing a little. "I will be. I'll visit and talk to the mom, be a kind of outreach support if she needs it."

"You're a good man, Ryan."

"It's my job."

"No, it's not just your job. I think it's all you."

They kissed, and when Jordan pulled back, Ryan was smiling a little and there was heat in his eyes.

"We should start now," Ryan said with confidence.

"Start what?"

"Sex."

"Now?"

Ryan kissed him and laughed into the kiss. "I think now is the perfect time." That was when his stomach rumbled. "But maybe we should eat something first. I have cold cuts and bread and stuff."

Jordan smiled up at him. "I could go for food." He couldn't stop himself from kissing Ryan again, and it was a long time before they made it to the small kitchen.

"I love your place," Jordan admitted as he cut up thick slices of chicken on his plate.

Ryan snorted. "A living room and a bedroom?"

"You have a microwave."

"And a kettle," Ryan deadpanned.

"And a refrigerator," Jordan added.

Ryan smiled at that. "I either eat at the office or with Saul in the main kitchen."

"It's—" Jordan glanced back at the photos on display, the comfy sofa, the magazines, the color on the walls. "—warm. I feel safe here." Although that could be because he was with Ryan. They were sitting on opposite sides of the small breakfast bar that separated the kitchen from the sitting room. "You're close to Saul?"

"Very. He's a good guy."

"What about your other brothers?"

"We're all close—overprotective idiots a lot of the time. I fell out with Eddie a while back after I fucked up, but we're okay now."

"How did you fuck up?"

"Long story short, his ex was a psycho, and so I suggested we background-check his new girlfriend, Jenny. Didn't go down so well. But now it turns out Jenny did a runner on him anyway when he mentioned the L-word and my nephew called her mom. He went and talked to her but she said she needed time to think."

Jordan felt sympathy. He'd never been in love before, not real, heart-pounding love, but to give your heart to someone only for it to be rejected had to be the worst thing ever. "Poor guy."

"Yeah. He's leaving the kids with me on Sunday so he can meet up with her and talk. The kids love her, and I like her, we all like her. But, you know, she'd be taking on a ready-made family. Hard."

"Very."

"What about you?" Ryan asked.

"What about me?"

"You're close to Micah?"

"It's a twin thing," Jordan said. "We're closer than close, which sounds weird now I said it."

"Do you have any other siblings?"

"None. My mom says that carrying the two of us for nine months was the best form of contraception ever. I know my dad wanted more kids, Mom told us so, but he died very young."

He immediately regretted bringing that up. Now he'd have to explain how his dad died and how many secrets his family held to themselves.

Ryan had apparently done his googling duties well. "Cancer, I saw that," he said. "I'm sorry."

Jordan's gaze dipped and he shrugged. "That's life." Given that Ryan had lost both of his parents, it wasn't the most diplomatic thing Jordan could have said. "Sorry," he mumbled at the end.

"So, about being in the closet... you can't tell me people don't know. People like Neil Patrick Harris and Matt Bomer, they're gay and they get parts. Isn't it okay to be gay now?"

Something twisted sickly inside Jordan, and he pushed it down with a great effort. "I'm not an A-list actor. I'm an ex-child star who leads made-for-TV romance movies—hetero romances. The kind of people who invest in me have 'standards.'" He air quoted to emphasize the word. "You can't have an openly gay actor playing the heterosexual lead unless they have the star power for the networks to get enough viewers who don't care about his sexuality."

"But you have your own company now. Doesn't that make it easier?"

Jordan shook his head, chewing on the last of his food and swallowing before answering. "This is year one. We're selling this movie to the network with the morality issues. Year five is when we'll film the script I'm writing. When we're big and successful and don't have to give a damn."

"And then you'll come out of the closet?" Ryan asked.

The question was the usual one that Jordan asked himself every day. People in the industry knew, but it had never become a problem as long as he kept himself under the radar, and that had never been an issue. He'd never met a man who made him want to walk down the road holding hands, or sit in a restaurant and stare stupidly into his lover's eyes.

Ryan was a first—Jordan's first. "I guess...," he said. "One day it won't be an issue."

Ryan picked up the plates and cutlery and moved them to one side, and then he leaned over the counter and kissed Jordan. "Your secret is safe with me."

They kissed lazily, and Jordan's words spilled out without control. "What if I didn't want you to keep it secret?"

Ryan looked confused, and then the confusion cleared. "Is that what you want? For someone to out you so you don't have to do it yourself?"

The question was soft, but there was real purpose in what he was saying. He was cutting right to the center of all the mess in Jordan's head with those few simple words. "No. Yes... no—fuck."

Ryan looked at him, no judgment in his expression, nothing but concern and affection. "Come on. I have movies and then bed."

"No dessert?"

Ryan patted his belly. "Need to stop eating dessert."

That wasn't the first time Ryan suggested he needed to watch what he ate, and Jordan couldn't understand it. He stopped Ryan with a hand to his chest as he moved past. "Why?"

A mix of emotions showed in Ryan's expression: resignation, laughter, confusion, and Jordan catalogued each one. And then Ryan shrugged as though he had no answer or was uncertain whether Jordan would understand. Then Ryan's hand went to his belly, just a brief movement, something anyone else might have missed.

In a smooth move, Jordan pushed up the worn T-shirt that Ryan had pulled on, up and over his head, twisting the material so his arms were pinned.

"Stay still," he said when Ryan attempted to move away. "Look at you," he said reverently, because that was how Ryan made him feel. "You're so big." He stood up on tiptoes and pressed a kiss to the tip of Ryan's nose, then his lips, and then he nudged him back against the counter where they'd just eaten. Ryan didn't argue; his expression remained relaxed. "And here—you're so sexy, the scent here—" He buried his nose against Ryan's throat and then kissed a trail down to the left nipple before turning his attention to the right. "You have the broadest chest, and I can just lie on you because I know you can take it. And you could probably carry me, couldn't you?" He looked up and met Ryan's dark gaze, leaving the question hanging.

"Maybe," Ryan said, then quirked a smile. "If there was a reward at the end of it."

"So, back to this." Jordan traced Ryan's muscles down to his hipbones and the intriguingly sexy V that led to heaven, and then he pressed the flat of his hand to Ryan's belly. "All these muscles and then there is this tiny soft part of you," he said and massaged circles on Ryan's belly and then lower to catch on the tip of his erect cock with each pass. "I love that you are this huge, sexy, strong man, but only I know you have softness here that I can kiss and nuzzle and rest my head on."

Jordan hoped to hell he was making this sound sexy. There was nothing like a man who could take him to orgasm, all toppy and hard, and then have a quieter side, a softer part that only Jordan would know about.

Actually, Jordan had never experienced anything like it. Clearly it was a new kink.

"Then," he continued, skimming past Ryan's cock, "there are your thighs, like freaking tree trunks. I bet you struggle to find a uniform to fit." He ran his hands back up those thighs to Ryan's groin, and he'd clearly pushed him too far.

Ryan wriggled out of the T-shirt prison. In one move he had Jordan in a fireman's lift, and he deposited him on the bed before pushing the door shut behind him. "Clothes. Off." He was brooking no argument.

And Jordan was only too happy to comply.

Ryan opened the drawer in the cabinet next to the bed, grabbed condoms and lube and dropped a bunch of them on the bed.

Jordan couldn't help the snort of laughter despite being so turned on that his cock ached. "We've only just… jeez. you're aware I'm thirty?"

"And like I said," Ryan teased. "I'm thirty-three, but it's a long night."

As Ryan pinned Jordan to the bed, he took the greatest care of him, slicking himself and pushing inside gradually, only stopping when he rocked deep inside and Jordan felt the tension turn to the exquisite fullness he loved.

And then Ryan began to move, leaning over, and kissing as he fucked into Jordan.

And Jordan was lost. He curled up and rested his feet on Ryan's hips, opening himself wider, wanting more.

Ryan moaned into the kiss. "So hot. You turn me inside out." He buried his face into Jordan's neck. "Get yourself off."

Jordan was happy to comply. His cock was trapped, slick against Ryan's belly, and he was so close. All it took was his hand tugging at his cock against Ryan's movements, and he was lost. He closed his eyes and came, feeling the rhythm of Ryan's thrusts change, become erratic. Then he too was coming, shouting Jordan's name at completion.

"Fuck…." Ryan groaned into Jordan's neck; everything felt so right.

So when he'd pulled out and cleaned up and twisted them so that Jordan was on top, sprawled on Ryan in his favorite place, Ryan gathered him close. He pulled up the covers; no words were needed.

And they slept.

CHAPTER 13

~ *Adam* ~

Adam stood patiently to one side of the stables, one hand holding Easy's reins, the other pushed into his pocket.

He'd been standing in this same place for twenty minutes while the crew arranged parts of the barn for filming, and every molecule of him was iced over. The only thing that was keeping him going was coffee and the apologies that people kept making every time they walked past him.

"I swear, five more minutes," Micah explained.

And as he'd done last time, Adam simply nodded and watched Micah scurry away. The sun was bright, the glare from the snow caused problems with these scenes, and one of the cameras had broken. At first it was going to be ten minutes, then another five, and then five more....

"Fucking freezing," Gabe cursed at his side.

The day was typical Montana, where the season couldn't decide how much of winter to cling onto. The snow had stopped falling, but the air was icy and pricked at exposed skin, despite the sun.

"You don't have to stay here," Adam said. Gabe had only arrived a few minutes ago, watching out for Lightning, who was restless and stamping at the hard ground. "I can take Lightning as well."

"No, I'm good," Gabe said without hesitation. He stamped his own feet and exhaled a cloud of white into the air. "How are things?" he asked after a moment's silence.

Same question, different setting. His best friend was forever checking he was okay, not quite over the shock of Adam landing back in their lives, even after this time.

Adam gave his usual response. "Things are fine."

"Saw Justin earlier."

"Uh-huh."

"He looked like shit, like he hadn't slept in a week."

Adam made a noncommittal noise and moved from foot to foot to encourage blood flow.

After a short pause, in which Adam assumed he was considering what to say, Gabe asked, "What is it with you two?"

"Who?"

"You and Justin, of course. Everything was going okay, but since Christmas it hasn't been the same."

Since Christmas, when all my new dreams seem like memories.

"You don't get to ask me questions, Gabe. Remember we agreed you wouldn't push?"

He felt instant guilt because this whole thing with Justin wasn't about memory loss—or at least he was pretending it wasn't.

Gabe huffed. "This isn't only you, this is Justin as well. You're avoiding each other."

"It's personal," Adam said with a quick glance at Gabe.

Gabe looked hurt, but it cleared quickly. He'd been the most supportive person at Crooked Tree apart from Ethan, reclaiming his position as one of the two best friends Adam had in his life. Not that he could remember much about that friendship; some flashes of his childhood, some stories he'd heard, and under all that, a feeling that he was close to Gabe and Justin.

He just couldn't get the images out of his head, of Justin in his dreams.

Then, hearing that he'd been Justin's target even though Justin hadn't known it was him? Adam had accepted that at face value one evening as they played cards, drank beer. They'd been a little tense, but they'd gotten the words into the open.

But the day after, things were no different, and the act that Justin and he were playing out—the one where they talked to each other in public, even stood to be in the same room as each other—was just that: a horrible, heartbreaking act.

Ethan was way past just being anxious about his brother and his lover. And Sam fretted about everything. Now Gabe was getting involved, stuck in the middle, as usual.

"What can I do to help?" Gabe asked. "Because I want to help. I'm here, and you can tell me anything."

Gabe was attempting to broker a peace, and that was fine on the surface. But what if there could never be peace between him and Justin now? What if forgetting all the good things he had with Justin meant that the bad things would consume him.

What if he only remembered things that meant he would hate Justin?

Why would his brain do that to him?

"Nothing," he said. Then he lied, just to make things easier. "We're okay, I promise. I'm just going through one of those memory things." He knocked shoulders with

Gabe. "I hope they hurry the fuck up filming this bit, I'm turning into an icicle."

Gabe smiled at him, and Adam relaxed and smiled back. *I can do this.*

"Ready, guys?" Micah appeared from the left and gestured for them to follow.

Lightning and Easy were starring in the movie, with Jordan's character talking to them in the barn. The heroine whose name Adam couldn't recall was to come in and talk about Jordan's character's place in her life. And through all of it, Easy and Lightning had to stand in the stables and look, in Micah's word, *horsey.*

As it turned out, the horses were wonderful doing their bit, and Adam got to watch the actors go through their paces.

Evidently this was a kissing scene. An *angry* kissing scene. There was arguing, with Jordan's character telling the heroine he was leaving the next morning and the heroine accusing him of leaving them on Christmas Eve, and what about that tree he'd promised her daughter they'd put up?

Adam couldn't recall if he liked romance movies from before-memory-loss, but he was enjoying the whole process, and when the director yelled "Cut" after a fifth take and the crew clapped, he joined in, as did Gabe.

There were some extra shots to be done, but the horses were okay to stay where they were, and that left Adam and Gabe free. The sky was darkening, and all Adam wanted to do was get back to his and Ethan's place to chill. So, he said goodbye to Gabe, who frowned and sighed dramatically.

"You *can* talk to me," Gabe repeated, "if you think no one else you approach is listening to you."

That broke Adam's heart. Gabe was assuming he was way down the list, and that was as far from the truth as possible. Gabe was the one smiling constant in his life. He never judged him or questioned him, or made him feel anything inside other than loved.

Even Ethan avoided things when they were together. And why wouldn't he? Justin was his brother, and Adam was this half-man with a non-functioning memory and an ability to shut people out.

"I'll always find you to talk to first," he said, and they did a half bro-hug with back patting. "You're never second best, Gabe."

Gabe cleared his throat, but his eyes looked suspiciously bright. He left quickly, and didn't look back.

Great. Now I'm fucking up friendships as well.

Adam walked in the opposite direction to Gabe, up the hill, with his hands deep in his pockets and his shoulders hunched against the cold, the beanie on his head pulled as low as he could get it while still able to see. He walked a well-trod path up past the last cabin, which the Todds lived in, and into the trees. Walking for the longest time until he finally reached Silver Pond and found the rock he liked to sit on.

He sat and unwrapped one of his scarves and laid it on the rock before clambering up and sitting cross-legged upon it.

And then he attempted to center himself as he'd been shown, focusing on creating an image in his head.

He chose the ranch he sometimes saw in his dreams, but it quickly changed and became the façade of a store, all glass and etched patterns. He opened the door.

The scent of the inside assaulted him.

"Hey, Jamie, you back for the coloring?"

James "Jamie" Mahone was his name while he was in witness protection; that was what everyone knew him as. He didn't know what his real name was—he'd lived another life he'd forgotten. But at the ranch he was Jamie, and that felt okay.

"I'm booked in for the ten appointment," he said.

Then he climbed the curved steps that led to the studio above, looking at the pictures of tattoos that lined the stairway: dark gothic crosses and the most delicate of flowers, scripted names and more than a few dragons.

"Be with you in five," Billy "Stretch" Molan called over, intent on completing whatever the young girl was having done to her shoulder.

From where Jamie stood, it looked like cat's paw prints and a cursive name.

He crossed to the window and looked down at the sidewalk below. A man was there, the one who'd been following him. Or at least in his more fanciful moments, he imagined the man was tracking him. Unless it was just coincidence that the guy had been in two different places at the same time as Adam. He had dark hair, almost black, and was scrolling through a phone, a cigarette held in the other hand.

"Okay, ready for you," Stretch called over.

Adam looked back to the station the artist was cleaning down and sanitizing. The girl had left.

How long had he been staring down at whoever was under the window? Or was time shortened in dreams? How was he contemplating that? Was he really awake?

"How are you?" Stretch asked him. *"Happy with the tattoo so far?"*

Jamie was very happy. The large expanse of design, a horse with the most exquisite details, was having secondary colors put on today, and he welcomed the buzz and heat and prickle of pain as Stretch completed it.

When he left, they said goodbye, and Jamie paused at the door. He hugged Stretch and thanked him for the horse. For the longest time, they stared at each other, and then Stretch cradled his face and kissed him.

"Call me," Stretch said.

Jamie lifted a hand and carded it through Stretch's hair, tugging him down for another kiss.

The kiss became more and the store faded away, and suddenly the man with the dark hair was right next to them.

"Fucking idiot, I told you, no!" the man snapped and pulled a gun.

And all Stretch said, in a small, quiet voice, was *"It's okay, Jamie. One day you'll know how I always felt."*

Adam's eyes flew open. He didn't know how much time had passed, but the clouds were darkening; he scrabbled for his cell phone to check. He'd actually been sitting here two hours. No wonder his ass was numb and he felt like ice inside.

He scrambled off the rock, stretched out his muscles, and winced. Stupid idea, sitting on a freaking rock in the cold. Thank God he'd layered his clothes this morning.

As he walked back down the hill, the darkness pulled at him and he felt sick and uneasy. He'd never recalled in such vivid detail the man who had inked his back, and now his heart knew: he'd wanted Stretch, may have had real affection for him; certainly Stretch had smiled at him as if they had secrets between them.

The man with the dark hair had killed Stretch.

The same man who killed the security guys at the ranch. Not Justin. Another man, watching and waiting... and not saying a fucking word.

Adam's stumbling steps turned into running, and he fell over roots hidden by the snow, crunched through ice, and slip-slid the last of the distance to the Todds' place.

He needed to tell someone, needed to explain before the memories faded.

He made it as far as the stables when the pain in his head slowed him to a walk. A group of movie people had gathered outside the stall; their laughter filled his head. He saw Jordan there, and the cracks in his head began to split. The pain was so intense he fell to his knees, and that was that.

Game over.

CHAPTER 14

~ Ryan ~

Ryan parked and hesitated for a moment before getting out of the car. He wasn't technically on duty or on call, but this wasn't exactly an official visit anyway. Aaron had phoned him after Jordan called for paramedics at Crooked Tree.

He climbed out of the car and pulled on his thick coat. Aaron had said he should go to the Allens' house, which was where Adam was after he'd collapsed. He hadn't done that in a long time—months.

Ryan knocked on the door and walked right in, the warmth of the cabin making his cold face prickle, and shrugged off his coat.

"In here," Sophie said.

Marcus stood behind her, looking like he'd rather be anywhere other than here. He wasn't the best at dealing with the whole Justin-Adam missing/returned/lack of memory situation. But Marcus had not long finished his first rounds of cancer treatment, and he was constantly tired.

Ryan tipped an imaginary hat to Sophie, who offered him a small smile in return. Hell, how bad was this if all Sophie could muster was a lackluster half-smile? He hadn't spotted Aaron's ambulance in the parking area, so clearly this hadn't been a medical emergency where he'd needed to stay.

He walked into the front room and everyone turned to stare at him. Adam on the couch, Ethan next to him, with an arm over Adam's shoulder. Sam and Justin by the window— Justin looking like the world had been knocked out from under him. No sign of Jordan, but that was okay; this was clearly a family thing going on here.

"Ryan? Why are you here?" Ethan asked. He wasn't accusing; he sounded genuinely confused.

"Aaron said I should come over," he said by way of getting someone, *anyone*, to talk to him.

"We're okay," Ethan said.

"No, we're not," Justin said. "It's a good thing Ryan is here, maybe he can mediate—"

"He's a sheriff, not a counselor," Ethan pointed out.

Justin shook his head. "He's a neutral party.

"Justin—"

Ryan interrupted as everyone began to talk. "Will someone tell me what happened?"

"I freaking collapsed again." Adam said tiredly. "It's as simple as that."

"But there's more," Ryan prompted.

Justin scowled at him; Sam looked like he was going to full-on cry, and Adam like a stiff wind would blow him over.

"I remembered kissing Stretch, okay!" Adam snapped, holding his head and wincing.

"Who is that?" Ryan asked.

"The tattoo artist who did the horse on his back," Ethan offered, supporting Adam with a hand on his arm.

Adam leaned into Ethan. "I remember a man killing him," he began. "And there's something else." He looked at Ethan and swallowed.

"Tell him," Ethan encouraged.

"Yeah, tell him what you remember," Justin snapped, derision in his tone.

"Shut up, Justin." Ethan made to stand.

Adam stopped him. "It's okay. I remember Justin being there both times."

"I wasn't there," Justin declared. "It wasn't me who killed them."

Sam placed a hand on his arm, as though holding Justin in place.

"Then how do you explain me recalling you there?" This time Adam sounded broken, and he hid his face in his hands. Ryan got the impression that he didn't want those memories in his head, or if they weren't memories, then images, or whatever you wanted to call them.

"I didn't know you were alive! I would have seen you if I'd been there."

"You were there, and you left me," Adam said. "At least, I think you did."

Silence.

Ryan had walked into the shitstorm of all shitstorms. "Guys—"

"Justin wouldn't ever have hurt you," Ethan reassured Adam, holding him closer.

But evidently it wasn't hard enough. Adam yanked free and stumbled to stand. "*Hurt me?*" he shouted. "He put me in danger and left me for dead when we were kids. Why stop there?"

And then he ran, before anyone could get ahold of him, and way before Ryan had the presence of mind to catch him as he dashed past.

The slamming of the door was a resounding stop to whatever had been going on in the room.

"Does someone want to explain?" Why was Ethan just standing there? "Ethan, aren't you going after him?"

"He won't talk to me," Ethan said. And to Ryan's horror, Ethan's eyes teared up. "He thinks I'll always choose Justin over him."

"Well, he's fucking wrong," Justin shouted. "You shouldn't ever choose me over him. I'm toxic." He grabbed Sam's hand, and for a second they looked at each other, Sam with a look of understanding, Justin with determination and a plea in eyes that were filled with pain.

As they left, Justin pressed a hand to Ethan's shoulder. But Ethan didn't look up at him.

There was damage being done here.

Finally it was Ryan and Ethan alone.

"Ethan, this has to stop," Ryan murmured. He didn't know what to say for the best, but this thing was spiraling out of control. Maybe there was value in Justin's idea that he should leave for a while.

Ethan shook his head, as if he'd reached the end of things and couldn't see what to do next.

Ryan knew one thing: Adam had run out of here without a coat, with pain etched into his expression, and Ryan had to find him. he pulled on his own coat, grabbing another from the peg, and left the cabin. There was no sign of Justin and Sam, no sign of Adam. Then inspiration hit and he half-jogged to the stables. And there was Adam, in with Easy.

Ryan slung the extra coat over Adam's shaking shoulders.

"Do you need to see a doctor?" he asked carefully.

Part of him was expecting Adam to turn around and punch him in the face. He didn't. He buried his face in Easy's mane, and he was definitely crying. Ryan was a sheriff, he was supposed to take away people's fears, make them feel safe, but he was doing a piss-poor job of it right then.

"Justin loves you...," he began. "If he'd realized you were alive—"

"I *know*," Adam sobbed. "I didn't mean what I said. He didn't leave me, and I know in my heart he wasn't there at the ranch to try and hurt me. But my head won't shake what I keep seeing."

"You should tell him that, Adam."

"He knows, but he just takes it when I shout at him, and when I say these things, he just stands there and takes it all, and I want him to shout back and defend himself and he doesn't!"

Ryan reached out a hand and touched Adam's shoulder, and Adam turned and curled into him.

"I got him," Ethan said from his side.

Ryan was happy to see him. Adam needed Ethan, not him, so he passed him over into his keeping.

Adam didn't argue, he just held Ethan tight, and Ryan backed away a little. Then he turned on his heels.

Next on his list, Justin.

Ryan found him with Sam, outside of Branches.

"I'm not good for him," Justin said simply when Ryan came to a stop next to him.

"You need to talk."

"I don't want to talk," he snapped. "I make it worse every time."

"Justin—"

"I'm going." Justin indicated the bag at his feet. "I need to give Adam some space here to heal, and I'm making things worse by staying. When my head is so messed up anyway, I need to go."

"You're running away," Ryan said.

Justin shook his head. "I've tried, but I'm no good for him like this. Okay? It's not running away—it's giving him time."

Ryan's gaze flicked to Sam and the bag he held in his hands. "Jesus, Sam, you're really doing this?"

"I'm going with Justin," Sam said without hesitation. "Nate and Marcus know, and I organized a manager. I go where Justin goes."

Justin glanced at Sam, and there was such need and love on his face that Ryan's chest tightened.

"What will you do?" Ryan asked. Because hell, this was their home.

"I have some money," Justin said. "We'll be okay, and we'll come back. For now, though, we need to let Adam heal, and I'm just fucking things up when he sees me every day."

Ryan held up a hand. Since when did he become the mediator here? But all he could think was that Justin and Adam needed to talk. *Really* talk. "That's not true—"

"This is a burner cell." Justin handed over a handset. "I'll call in every so often, but if you need me, if *Adam* needs me, then call. Tell Ethan I'll be in touch."

"Justin, this is stupid. He says he wants you to argue back, to make him see—"

"I can't, Ryan. I've done enough damage."

"Justin, you have to see that Adam is transferring all his anger and loss onto you because he absolutely trusts you love him unconditionally. Because you let him."

Justin half smiled. "I'd take it all if it meant he was okay. And I will always, always come back for him. Just let him have this time."

Ryan pocketed the cell, and watched as they walked over the bridge to the parking lot and climbed into Justin's car. He waited until the car vanished around the corner and into the night before letting out a noisy sigh.

Shit.

"He's gone, then." A voice came from behind, and Ryan turned to see Gabe. "He said he might, just to give Adam some space."

"That's stupid," Ryan snapped. "If Justin told the truth about what happened, and Adam could listen to him, and then they clear the air...."

Gabe shrugged. "It's not that easy. With Adam recalling all this information and not being able to get a clear head? I don't blame Justin for leaving for a while. I think it's very brave of him, actually."

"This is fucked up," Ryan said with feeling. "I'm the sheriff here, yet I have no control over anything."

Gabe clapped him on the shoulder. "Sheriff or not, Ry, there's nothing else any of us can do tonight. Night."

"Night," he said by rote, then walked back to his car and belted up, giving the engine time to warm up the cab. And he considered just how close he was to Jordan here. He could follow the track down to the Forest Cabins; he knew which one Jordan was sharing with Micah and Angie.

Would Jordan want to see him? He was undoubtedly holed up running lines, or whatever actors did on their downtime, and anyway, they were due to see each other tomorrow at eight at Ryan's place.

Still, he guessed it wouldn't hurt if he drove down there and parked. Then, after pulling out his cell, he sent off a quick text.

At Crooked Tree after some drama. Need coffee.

There, that was okay, wasn't it? Or was it too demanding? He backspaced, paused, then retyped the exact same message. But would Jordan get that he was here at Crooked Tree, with the shitty cell reception? His cell only had two bars as it was.

He amended the text and considered it, realizing he was channeling his inner teenager and angsting over a simple message. In the end he pressed Send and waited. Thank God for two bars.

The answer was quick and to the point. *I have coffee, get down here.*

Sighing with relief, Ryan drove down the narrow track and parked by the cabin they were using as a set. The place was in darkness, but the tents were still there, empty of people. Evidently the evening shoot had come to an end. A security guy sat in a car, drinking coffee, and after a quick check, waved Ryan past.

This wasn't a Hollywood movie set with tons of security, but Ryan was pleased to see someone down here keeping an eye on the set-up.

He walked the short distance to Cabin 8. As Ryan stepped onto the path to the front door, it opened and Jordan came out. He wasn't wearing a coat, but that didn't stop him meeting Ryan halfway and kissing him in the dark.

"Come in," he said when they separated.

"Is this okay? I was just up at Crooked Tree and—"

Jordan cut off the question with another kiss and then tugged him inside, shutting the door behind them, then helping Ryan out with his coat.

They kissed again by the coats, again in the hallway farther in, and by the front room door. They only separated when Jordan pushed open the door.

Micah and Angie were curled up on the sofa, and in the background, an old episode of *Friends* was showing on the TV.

"Ryan's here," Jordan announced. "We'll be in my room."

Micah sketched a wave and then, with a raised eyebrow in comment, picked up the remote and turned up the volume on the television.

"Ass," Jordan said, good-naturedly.

He grabbed two beers and headed along the long corridor and opened the last door. Jordan flipped on the light, and it revealed a large bedroom with a half bath leading off it. The bedding was navy, the furniture sturdy, the drapes pulled, and Jordan turned on a small bedside lamp before turning off the main light.

"Is Adam okay? He just crumpled to the ground and fell like a sack of potatoes. I called a paramedic."

"He's okay, sometimes…. It's a long story." Ryan couldn't contemplate where to start explaining all of this. "Let's just say the whole story would make for an intriguing screenplay."

"You want to watch something? I have my laptop."

Ryan slipped off his shoes and then gathered Jordan up in his arms. Stepping back, he allowed his weight to tip them onto the bed. Jordan sprawled across him. "No," he said. "I want to just lie here and kiss you. A lot."

"I can get with that plan," Jordan murmured against his throat.

And they kissed for the longest time, talking between kisses until the kissing became more urgent and Jordan slid down his body. Abruptly, Ryan couldn't think of anything he wanted to say, and lost himself to making love.

After, they lay in each other's arms, conversing quietly. Ryan loved this part of sex, and he didn't get it very often. Just lying with your lover in your arms, chatting about everything and nothing. Somehow they'd landed on talking about films, a nice safe subject that Jordan was passionate about and one that Ryan was happy to know more about.

"What happens after you've shot all the separate scenes like the one I watched?" Ryan asked. "Do you have to sit in a room and splice together all the bits of film?"

"No, everything is digital. I mean the rushes—the separate parts are digitized."

"And then what happens?"

"You get an editor, and he or she takes all the bits and creates an edit decision list. They'll read the script, look at the rushes, and from that information, cut the movie according to their opinion of what makes the story better."

"They mess with your story? Doesn't that piss you off?"

"No, they make it better. Well, mostly they do." Jordan chuckled and pressed his face into Ryan's neck.

"Shouldn't an editor be telling you what to shoot in the first place?"

"Oh, he did. We had a whole list of the kind of things he wanted filmed from the script."

"Like?"

"We have a fight coming up—the cops arrive at the ranch and they have an arrest warrant for my character, and he doesn't take it well. Gets into a fight with one of the cops, who has a thing for the heroine. They end up in the water."

"The water? Here? In this temperature? Fuck, Jordan, you'll kill yourself."

Jordan looked up and smiled, pressing a soft kiss to Ryan's chin. "Anything for my art."

Ryan grunted his displeasure and then decided to change the subject. Jordan wasn't his to worry about. If he got hypothermia, it wasn't on Ryan.

Please don't get hypothermia.

"How long does it take to edit?" he asked to stop himself getting lost in worrying.

"Ten weeks or so, and they make different drafts: the rough cut, the answer print. When you're happy with the visuals, you need a sound editor."

"It's kind of complicated."

"Yeah." Jordan shifted a little so they were face to face, and then he wriggled into what seemed to be his favorite position, lying half on and half off Ryan's chest. Ryan moved his hands and rested them on Jordan's ass, and Jordan smiled up at him. "Very complicated," he continued. "Two months after we finish filming, music has to be added, and we cut dialogue tracks, sort out sound effects, make cue sheets for the mix, that kind of thing."

"And then you're done?"

"No. Sometimes we have to go back and lip-sync and loop dialogue that wasn't sharp and clear. And the Foley artist puts things like the noise of footsteps and certain other sound effects into your movie."

"Wait, you have someone in charge of footsteps?" The filmmaking process sounded way too complicated to be fun, but Jordan seemed to thrive on it if the grin he wore was anything to go by.

"And doors, and hooves, and crunching snow, and *oofs* and punches for the fight scenes."

They kissed, and Ryan had the feeling he could get used to this, lying in bed, loose from making love, just chatting about his man's day. He hadn't mentioned his day, nothing past the word *drama*, but he didn't want to bring his thoughts about all that here into their bed. Not yet. He just wanted hugs and loving.

I want that so bad.

"There's more," Jordan said. "Am I boring you? I can stop."

Ryan didn't want to admit he could listen to Jordan talking all day, but sue him, he did. Stopping meant that they might have no reason to be snuggled under the covers and holding each other close. "No, go on."

"A musician composes music—the score—for setting the mood or foretelling a change in scene. Music is really important because it can change the way a person connects to the story, the emotional responses they have."

Kind of like how angels were singing when I was inside you, Ryan thought fancifully. He didn't say that, though; he wasn't an idiot and he didn't want to be laughed at.

Big, strong, and tall sheriff getting all soft and mushy over good sex. *Nope, not happening.*

Jordan continued his explanation. "We put everything together. All the tracks of sound are layered to create a feeling of depth. Then there are the main titles, and the crawl titles at the end are all added to the master file, and finally you end up with a digital cinema package. There's also marketing, stills work, posters, sound bites, plus the inevitable interviews and trailers."

"So basically what you are saying is that the process is a long one and I have severely underestimated what goes into making a movie."

Jordan chuckled and moved a little again. All the wriggling was making Ryan hard, and when he realized Jordan was just as interested, it was like he was eighteen again.

Only as he was holding Jordan to him and they were kissing did he realize two things: Jordan had made him forget everything, and he wanted Jordan in his life on a permanent basis.

Which meant he was opening himself up to heartbreak when Jordan and the crew left.

CHAPTER 15

~ *Jordan* ~

The news hit the Internet first. A few Twitter posts that used the hashtag #JordanGay. He didn't even notice them until a few people actually referenced his Twitter handle in retweets.

"Rumors, that's all it is," Micah reassured him as he scrolled through the tweets on his cell.

None of them were particularly bad. No one said anything awful; one or two said it was obvious, but most of them were just passing on the gossip.

And then the photo appeared.

Him and Ryan in the tent. Kissing.

Pressed up against each other, with Ryan holding him still and Jordan with his hands in Ryan's hair. The way his head was tilted, it was obviously him, but Ryan's face was hidden. However, the bulk of him and the fact he was in uniform was a dead giveaway of his identity.

Jordan wasn't sure what to freak out about first—the photo itself, Ryan being in it, the fact he was being publicly outed, or that someone on the crew had taken the photo in the first place.

He felt sick, and he sat down on the sofa as his legs gave way under him. "We need to… I have to… Ryan."

Micah took the chair opposite. "First we find out who took the photo. Right?"

"But Ryan…."

"He's next on my list. The news isn't going to spread, J. You're not Brad Pitt."

Jordan wasn't concentrating and got confused. "What?"

"A-list, okay? You're not A-list. There's no need to think this will go viral. People won't care."

"The channel buying this movie might care. Jesus, Micah, this could have them backing out of taking it from us, and we're done. All the money you and I put into this, all the time... this could destroy Darby Films."

"Get a grip," Angie snapped from next to him and snatched the phone from his hand. "Most people in the industry know you're gay," she said. "This is a couple of tweets about a guy who was once in a kid's show. It will blow over."

Jordan wasn't sure what to be more focused on, that he'd been consigned by both his brother and Angie as B-list, or that the photo was out there, or hell, that Angie just blurted out that the industry was aware of his orientation.

"And Ryan is already out, right?" she continued. "He'll get some local notoriety for a while, and then it will be done."

Only it wasn't so easy.

The photo didn't go viral and mostly vanished after a couple of days, and thank God no one from the channel buying the film actually called and pulled out. But by the time the photographer had been identified—an intern who currently stood shakily in front of him—Jordan had garnered attention from way too many people. Including a text from Ryan with the ominous words *We need to talk.*

"Why?" he asked Shawna. The slip of a thing was in her college gap year and had seemed so into everything on set, always zipping here and there, 100 percent invested.

"It's okay, I'm going," she said, her blue eyes bright with unshed tears.

She held herself upright, obviously holding her emotions in check, and Jordan had expected something different. Crying, apologies, or anger maybe, but not this quiet acceptance.

"You want some hot chocolate?" he asked, inspired.

Seemed like she was going to fall over if she didn't sit down. Her eyes widened and he didn't wait for her answer, getting two hot chocolates and gesturing her to follow him to the table.

Shawna sat down and folded her hands on the tabletop in front of her.

"Tell me what happened," Jordan encouraged.

"I wouldn't know where to start," she said.

"From the beginning is always good."

"My brother is gay," she said. Like that explained it, or justified what she'd done.

"Okay, and?" Jordan encouraged.

"He's at college, his first year, and he was bullied in school. I've been telling him about you, and how you seem happy and you have a career and it doesn't scare you that you're gay, just that you don't make it public. I sent the photo to him because he didn't believe me." She cupped her hands around the chocolate. "I'm sorry. I didn't know his stupid asshole of a friend would share it."

"That's what asshole friends tend to do," Jordan said.

"I know that now, and I understand I need to go. I won't tell anyone anything, and I promise I regretted it as soon as I took it. I didn't send it for days after I took it, and then one night after he called me and he was crying, and it just… broke my heart. I sent it to him."

The words tumbled out, but she still didn't cry, although she'd made her lip bleed where she'd bitten it and the tears were there waiting to fall.

"You need to respect my privacy," Jordan said. Because hell, what else could he say? "But I don't want you to leave, and we're dealing with the situation."

Shawna stared at him blankly, as if she couldn't believe what he'd just said. "Mr. Darby—"

"Jordan," he corrected her. "From what I'm told, you're doing a really good job, and don't think I didn't notice how hard you work. I'm not going to get rid of you because of one photo." He sighed heavily and sat back in the seat. "Anyway, maybe this is what I needed to happen."

"Mr.—Jordan, I'm genuinely sorry."

"Shawna, thank you. And tell your brother if he needs to talk to someone, I'm here."

She left, chocolate in hand, still looking shell-shocked.

Jordan didn't move until Micah slid into the seat she'd left.

"You let her stay, and you understood why she did it, and you even reassured her."

"She tell you that?"

Micah huffed a laugh. "No, she just looked at me and I used my supertwin sense. I knew you'd crumble when she cried."

"She didn't cry. Nowhere near it. She told me about her brother."

"Zach."

"You know her brother's name?"

"He's her next of kin," Micah shrugged.

Jordan felt suddenly sentimental. He may be the front of this company, but without Micah running everything behind the scenes, he'd struggle. "I love you. You know that, right? Without you, Darby wouldn't be a thing."

Micah wrinkled his nose. "Back at you."

"What are we going to do if the channel tells us they don't want the movie? What if I start trending for real and no one buys into the gay man playing the straight lead?"

"Then we'll sell it somewhere else. It's a good, solid Christmas romance."

"And if it doesn't sell?"

"Stop it Jordan, okay? Let's just go with the flow here."

But that was easier said than done, and now a whole day had passed and the channel had made their concerns known. They weren't too worried, but used their bargaining position for more of Jordan's time with publicity leading up the film's release. Jordan felt like he was getting off lightly and agreed. As of today everything was still on track. After all, it was only March, and the release was eight months away. A long time for a tweet and a picture to die down.

He just wished he didn't have the specter of Ryan wanting to talk hanging over him. He still had to explain all this to Ryan—and Ryan was probably going to kill him.

As if on cue, "Ryan's here," Angie called from outside catering, and Jordan groaned and scrubbed at his eyes. Could the day get any worse?

He went out to meet Ryan, who was walking toward him. *How the hell do I explain this?*

When they met, Ryan took his hand and tugged him into the trees, rounding on him and cradling his face.

"Are you okay?" he asked.

"What?"

"Rookie showed me a photo he found online. Are you okay?"

And right there and then, Jordan fell in love with Ryan, the man with compassion on his face and understanding in his eyes.

Love. Right into it. Head first.

Jordan cleared his throat to stop himself blurting it out. "I'm more worried about you."

"Me?"

"They only have to look at the photo and see your uniform, and they'd know it was you."

"Who?" Ryan looked confused, and then the confusion turned to something softer. "I'm not hidden away, and no one has an issue with their sheriff being gay. Hell, they knew that when they voted me in. I don't care who knows it's me, and if anyone has concerns, then that's their issue, not mine."

The words made Jordan's worry lift a little. If Ryan could be so calm, so worried about Jordan that he came here to find him? *I don't know what to do with this feeling.*

"Are you sticking around?" he asked. Ryan was in uniform and chances were Jordan was just a stop in his day.

"I can." He stepped back a little and considered Jordan, who was still in his character clothes.

"I'm done in about ten. We've wrapped my scenes today. I could meet you at the cabin."

"How about you come back to mine? I have my niece and nephew staying tonight for family dinner, and you can meet my brothers."

This seems real. This will be me meeting Ryan's extended family—a step forward into the unknown where there'll be no going back.

"You don't have to, though. We could just meet up tomorrow like we planned."

Caution laced Ryan's tone, and abruptly Jordan didn't want to hear that; he wanted the soft affection from his big bear of a man. "I would love that. I'll meet you at yours."

Which was how Jordan found himself at the table in the Carter kitchen above the bar, with three of Ryan's brothers. Saul, he knew. The eldest of the five boys, he was a cool guy with a wicked sense of humor under the serious layers. Jason was the firefighter, cute and very funny. He was in lust with a girl called Becky, a veterinary assistant he'd helped out with a gas leak at her place two weeks back. She frequently texted him pictures of herself and various animals she'd dealt with at the surgery. Which, of course, was something Ryan and Saul teased him about.

Aaron was quiet, the odd one out, the middle sibling and a paramedic. He also seemed to be the peacemaker, and as a result, he took the fence on everything. When Ryan teased Jason, it was Aaron who stopped him; when Jason teased back about the photo on Twitter, Aaron kicked him under the table.

Jordan only knew that because Aaron missed and kicked him instead. "Ow!"

"Sorry," Aaron apologized, but at the same time he couldn't help a twitch of laughter from quirking his mouth.

Then there was Jake and Milly, as cute as kids could be, young, sweet, and obviously loving their uncles. What was more obvious was that the four men spoiled them completely. They planned trips out, sleepovers, a ride in Uncle Ryan's sheriff's car, another in Uncle Aaron's ambulance—although both uncles explained they wouldn't be able to go out *for really real*.

Which just left Eddie, the second eldest, who wasn't there. Eddie, the father of the two kids, who were.

"You can go watch television," Saul said to them. "Take the dessert."

Milly immediately stood up. "C'mon, Jake. Uncle Saul wants to talk about Daddy." She sounded so grown up.

No one made a sound until Jake and Milly, with plates of chocolate cake, disappeared through a door to the left of the kitchen, presumably to some kind of sitting room.

"Are we?" Saul asked.

"Are we what?" Ryan replied, cutting two slices of cake and passing one to Jordan.

"Talking about Eddie?"

"Jenny," Aaron said gently. "We should talk about Jenny. I like her, the kids like her, and hell, Eddie is in love with her."

"I think she's scared," Saul said with a loud sigh. "Of the family, of being an instant mom."

Jordan followed the conversation as best he could. Eddie liked Jenny. Eddie told Jenny he loved her and Jenny ran.

The brothers discussed and argued, and no one came to any conclusion.

Then Jordan had an idea that he thought had some merit. "You should just tell her she wouldn't be on her own. That all four of you, and Eddie, would be there for the kids, and that she wasn't marrying them, just Eddie, and that she could ease into things slowly."

All four of them looked at him as if he had said something completely wrong—but then Saul nodded.

"She's an only child who looks after her dad. Coming into *this*—" Saul swept a hand to indicate the whole table. "—would be overwhelming."

"Shit," Jason said, "you think that's it?"

The door to the kitchen opened. Another man walked in, who looked so much like Ryan that Jordan knew this was the missing Eddie, and behind him, clutching his hand, was a beautiful woman with raven hair and green eyes. She looked wary, but she didn't pull away from Eddie's hand.

The brothers at the table all started talking at once.

"We'll look after the kids."

"We love the kids, they'll be fine, you'll have space."

"Eddie loves you, he will make this work."

"Jenny, we'll help, and you'll never know that—"

"*Guys!*" Eddie interrupted loudly.

Everyone stopped talking and watched as Eddie slipped an arm around Jenny's waist.

"I need you to look after Jenny," Eddie said. "I have to talk to the kids."

Saul stood and offered his seat, and Jenny sat, right opposite Jordan. They exchanged smiles.

"I'm Jenny," she said.

"Jordan," he said and extended a hand over the remains of the chocolate cake.

Saul scraped one of the kids' chairs to a new spot and sat down, looking faintly ridiculous on the higher seat.

And then everyone had absolutely nothing to say.

"He asked me to marry him, again," she said.

Still no answer; everyone looked at her expectantly.

"I said yes."

"Thank God," Saul said with feeling, and that opened the floodgates. By the time Eddie came back through the other door, with Jake in his arms, clinging like a monkey, and Milly near dancing at his side, it was obvious both kids were happy with the proceedings. And given the way Jenny scooped up Milly into her hold, it seemed she was equally as happy.

"When can we find my dress?" Milly asked as she twirled Jenny's hair around her finger.

"How about the same time I get mine?"

Jordan lifted his glass, the orange juice nearly gone. "A toast to Eddie and Jenny," he declared, and Ryan and his brothers followed suit.

"When is the wedding?" Aaron asked.

"June, we think." Eddie looked at Jenny as he spoke, and she smiled and nodded.

"June," she agreed.

"Saul?" Eddie began and looked at the others in turn. Some message passed between them, an agreement of sorts. "Will you be my best man?"

Saul swallowed the sip of drink he'd just taken, seemingly fighting all the emotions at once—he was overwhelmed. "I'd be honored," he said. And then he toasted. "To a June wedding."

"You'll be next," Jason teased Ryan, who colored and stared down at the table.

"Yep, just not sure who wears the dress," Eddie pointed out, and then huffed in pain and glared at Aaron, who'd evidently done more of his kicking under the table. "What?" Eddie asked innocently and then shrugged. "About time all of you settled down."

Eventually, Eddie and Jenny left with the kids, and congratulations followed them out the door. Then Jason, who said he was on early duty, left with Aaron close behind. Saul excused himself to the bar, and only when everyone else had left did it occur to Jordan that no one had done the dishes.

He rolled up his sleeves and poured water onto soapsuds, swirling the water around with a brush.

Ryan cleared the table, coming up behind him and wrapping his arms around Jordan's waist, resting his chin on his shoulder.

"Sorry," he said, "my brothers are assholes. Well, some of them. Eddie and Jason mostly."

Jordan turned off the water and turned in Ryan's arms. "They're all awesome," he said, cupping Ryan's face with his wet hands and grinning up at him when he winced and cursed. "You're still my favorite, though."

Yep. Ryan was the very best.

"Will you come back from LA for the wedding?" Ryan asked, his tone wary, a little nervous.

This was the moment that Jordan made some kind of commitment to the man who'd stolen all the parts of his heart. But what if Ryan didn't actually want him back? What if this was just a month of sex and fun that would naturally end next week when the movie was done?

"Do you want me to?"

Ryan kissed him then, a gentle kiss, and whispered against Jordan's lips. "*Yes.*"

Jordan's heart lifted and he deepened the kiss for a moment before pulling back. "Then I'll be here."

CHAPTER 16

~ *Ryan* ~

Frankie rapped her knuckles on Ryan's open door and he sat back in his chair and smiled at her. She didn't look happy, and the last time that had happened was when their last rookie had broken the photocopier.

"What's wrong?" he asked, as his smiled dropped.

"Just had young Nate from Crooked Tree on the phone, seems like there's a strange car abandoned at the edge of the road into the ranch."

Ryan immediately stood. Why was Frankie standing there like this wasn't hugely important? After what had happened the last time, an abandoned car needed handling with way more urgency. "I'm on it."

"You don't need to rush." She looked at her nails. "Seems the driver was taking a rather circuitous walk to the filming area and Adam may have hit him."

"Hit him how?"

Frankie made a fist and bopped herself on the nose. "Like that."

"I'm going. Tell them I'll be there as soon as I can."

"I already did. The man, and Adam and Nate, and probably all those hot cowboy types are at the restaurant there. Yum, so sexy."

A grandmother. And she was sashaying out of his room on the word *sexy*. Ryan was somewhat used to her behavior by now… as long as he didn't think about it too much.

He didn't break any speed records to get to Crooked Tree, but he certainly didn't hang around. Nate met him in the parking lot, his face grim.

Ryan nodded in greeting. "So, who is it?"

"The guy won't give us his name, and Adam has moved on to intimidation. You need to settle him down."

Ryan jogged alongside Nate and burst into Branches.

Jay was there, and Adam with his arms folded, in a pose that attempted to exude threat but actually came over as scared. He had blood on his cheek, and he was stiff with tension.

And the man Adam had allegedly hit? He was in a chair, held in place with rope of some sort, and he was bleeding.

"Thank God!" the man began, his eyes widening as Ryan burst in, and his features morphing from scared to smug. "You need to arrest this man." He attempted to indicate Adam, but with his hands secured to the chair, it ended up being more of a waggle of his fingers. "He hit me."

"Untie him," Ryan said. Whatever had happened he wasn't talking to the guy while he was tied up.

"He's not armed," Adam said as he slipped the knot and released the stranger.

All Ryan could think was *Jeez, Adam's not only hit the guy, but he's frisked him as well?* The day was going from bad to worse. Adam had been on the edge since he'd come home, and he was maybe worse since Justin left. Hell, it was as if he was channeling Justin.

The man held out a hand and introduced himself. "Thomas Ivory."

Ryan shook his hand, because he couldn't not do that; he was the law, after all, and trying to be impartial. But something about that name was ringing all kinds of bells.

"Can you tell me what happened here?"

"He was trespassing, with a camera, by the filming," Adam snapped.

Ryan held up a hand to stop him. "You should go outside," he said and then escorted Adam out of the door. "Leave it for now. And call Jordan and tell him a Thomas Ivory is here."

Adam nodded, already moving toward the office for the radio to contact the set. Ryan sighed deeply. He'd placed the name, and the man in there was the journalist Jordan had warned him about, the one writing the book about the Darby family. But he was also a citizen, and Ryan needed to handle this the right way. Plus, he wasn't sure Adam would be up to appearing in court against Ivory.

Fuck.

After pasting on his official expression, he went back into the restaurant.

"Sir, please explain to me what happened here."

Thomas flicked at his jacket as if he was removing dirt, then pressed a napkin from the closest table to his nose, checking for blood when he pulled it away. Ryan didn't mention all the blood down his white T-shirt.

"I'm lucky he didn't break my nose," Ivory said, a little nasally.

Ryan ignored him for the moment; he needed to get to the bottom of this, but he also wanted to wait for Jordan to get here. "Start from the beginning."

"I was birdwatching," Ivory began. "I parked my car on the road and went into the woods, saw a horse, and approached the rider who was on a trail there."

"The man you say hit you."

"That man, yes. He hit me."

"He hit you. Why would he do that?"

Ivory looked down and away. "I have no idea."

He was lying, obviously. "So, you're alleging that your assailant randomly hit you for no reason while you were birdwatching?"

Ivory bristled. "He believed I was trespassing. He threatened me, even when I explained I was taking photos and I was sorry for straying onto private land. So I defended myself."

"You hit him?"

Ivory narrowed his eyes. "As I said, I was defending myself."

There was calculation in his brown eyes, as though he'd been in this situation before and knew how to get out of it.

"I won't press charges." Ivory did that whole brushing-at-his-jacket thing and straightened it. "We'll just let this go."

"I need to see some ID and your camera," Ryan said, playing the hunch that could solve this.

The ID was easily handed over, but Ivory seemed less than happy to give up his camera. "There's nothing on there that you need to see," he said.

"No problem," Ryan said and watched him relax. "I'll escort you and the man you are accusing to the sheriff's office, and we can discuss the situation there."

Two could play at this game of bluffing. If Ryan was right—and he had a feeling he was—then there was no way Ivory would push this as far as actually following through on the report.

"I said to this man that there was no need to worry the sheriff," Ivory hedged.

"Nate? You want to give me your side of this?"

"Adam radioed in, said he had a trespasser and needed assistance because the man was hostile." Ryan nodded in encouragement. "I took the quad up there and found this man on the ground, with Adam sitting on his chest. I noticed the blood on his face and also on Adam's. He was violent once Adam released him, so we called you."

"Violent?"

"Started shouting about his rights and so on." Nate crossed his arms over his chest and quirked an eyebrow. "Thought you should get involved."

The door flew open and Jordan arrived in a flurry of cold air and temper. "Adam said you needed me." He stopped in front of Ryan and looked him right in the eyes. "What happened?"

Ryan simply gestured to where Ivory stood; he catalogued the expression on Jordan's face. Shock, horror, anger, and then absolute ice.

"You know this man?" Ryan asked Ivory directly.

"No. Yes—no," Ivory hedged.

"Which is it?" Ryan pushed.

"Yes. He's an actor," he admitted.

Jordan stepped a little closer, but Ryan put a hand on his arm to stop him.

"And one with a restraining order against you," Jordan said.

Ivory deflated, and Ryan went into sheriff mode.

By the time Ivory left the property, his camera had been wiped.

He had a parting word for Jordan, though, and it was as if he forgot Ryan was right there. "I saw the photo. I know what you are, and I know you're your father's son. Believe me, we all know how your dad really died."

Jordan didn't move or react until Ivory left; Ryan and he watched him go, walking through the parking lot to the road and his car, without a backward glance.

Then Ryan turned to his lover, wanting to grab him and hold him close, seeing the desolation on his face. "Jordan?"

"Thank you," Jordan murmured.

"What is he trying to create about your dad?"

Jordan pushed his hands in his pockets and hunched into his coat. "That dad was a depraved predator in a climate where sex was handed out at parties like favors. That there was something in the way he died, drugs, AIDs, you name it, he's mentioned it."

Ryan reached out and placed his hands on Jordan's arms. "He had cancer. That is all people need to know." He didn't care if it was true or not. Jordan's father had died, as many young men in the industry had at that time. It was a lifetime of yesterdays, and nothing would be served by hashing things out now.

"I don't even know why we don't just send the medical records out. Dad had cancer, but he did sleep around a lot, cheated on my mom. You add in the gay son and suddenly there's no level people like Thomas Ivory won't go to," Jordan said quietly. "Micah and I don't care, we'd release the records tomorrow, but Mom, she doesn't feel we need to prove anything to anyone. She says—and she's probably right—that it would look like we had something to prove, and we don't. Dad was Dad, and that was it."

"Jordan—"

"I'm tired of it. All of it. Keeping secrets, hiding myself."

Ryan tightened his grip and desperately wanted to haul Jordan in for a kiss, but they were in the open, and he was in uniform, and hell, that could just muddy the waters after what had just happened. "I'll be here if you ever need me. You know that, right?"

Jordan looked right at him, a smile on his lips. "That's what makes me think I can be different," he said. "You make me feel stronger and more certain."

Ryan didn't move for the longest time. Seeing the ugliness that was an integral part of Jordan's world made him feel on edge and unbalanced.

He wanted to be the strong one; wanted to be there for Jordan. Jordan just had to let him know he needed him, and Ryan would be all over that immediately.

"I need to focus on the next scenes. Listen, do you want to stay to watch the fight scene being filmed?" Jordan asked.

Ryan checked his watch. Midday had rolled on to 1:00 p.m., and he was officially off the clock. "Yeah, I'd like that."

He watched in awe the mechanics of setting up what would be no more than a minute on film. Jordan was in his character's clothes, but under the loose shirt, he wore a cut-off wetsuit. The water was churning today, some of the snow melt increasing the volume, and Ryan didn't want his lover in there.

Hell, his first instinct was to demand they cut the scene from the film.

The safety measures included a lifeguard in a full wetsuit, with ropes and pulleys forming a net the other side of the bridge, well out of sight. Ryan guessed it was in case one of the actors floated off down the river. That freaked him out enough that he went back to his car, removed his watch, weapon and his phone from his body, and secured them away in his weapons locker. Just in case there was trouble. Because sue him, he would be the first one in the freaking water.

There was a foam barrier tied down to change the flow of the water a little, taking the pressure off. The actors involved, Jordan, and a man in a cop's uniform were listening avidly to a woman Ryan guessed was the stunt coordinator.

"He'll be okay," Micah said from his side, startling Ryan and making him realize just how involved he was in worrying about Jordan.

There was a paramedic on standby—not Aaron, but someone assigned to the movie. Ryan wished Aaron was here because he was a very strong swimmer.

"Why isn't Jordan wearing the full wetsuit?" he asked Micah under his breath.

Micah looked at him like it was obvious. "Because his shirt in this scene is low-cut."

"Then he should be wearing a turtleneck sweater. And a beanie."

Micah huffed a laugh. "That won't work. We need the cop to fight Jordan's character, and for Emma's double to fall in the water trying to save him." Micah waved at a woman, who from the back looked a lot like the ten-year-old playing Emma, but from the front was a short, forty-year-old woman.

"They won't let Emma in the water, right?"

"Nope, it's all stunt work and the magic of the movies." Micah gestured at the water. "And we'll take breaks."

"This is crazy, stupid, and dangerous," Ryan muttered. "And I don't like it."

Micah elbowed him. "This is the only way for Jordan to get the effect he wants. It's a pivotal scene in the film, where Jordan's character becomes the hero of the story instead of a protagonist."

"He's a crazy fucker," the lifeguard said from Ryan's other side.

And that didn't bode well at all.

Ryan bit back his instant need to call a halt to the proceedings citing some long-forgotten code of policing. This was Jordan's job, and he needed to respect the man for putting himself through such a horrible experience while taking every possible precaution.

"Why doesn't Jordan have a body double?" he asked.

"Too many close-ups," Micah said.

The first scene was set, the two characters brawling on the side of the bank. From this angle it looked like the punches were actual hits, but as the fight moved, they were obviously choreographed near hits. Didn't make Ryan wince any less, though.

That scene took five takes, and then it was the water.

"Action!" Micah called.

The fight moved to the water, and with how well Ryan knew Jordan's facial expression, he could tell the fear was real. And the cold? Jesus, it must be freezing. Angie stood ready with space blankets, and everyone hoped this would be one take.

It was. Whoever had choreographed the fight had done their job, the body double for Emma was perfect, and suddenly Jordan and the cop were working together to rescue her. Once they grabbed her, all three climbed onto the bank, with Jordan falling to his knees and the cop slumping on the ground. They delivered some dialogue that Ryan couldn't hear from where he was, and then Micah yelled "Cut!"

The flurry of movement was impressive. Space blankets, heaters, people helped to a tent to strip and warm up.

"That's our boy," Micah said proudly.

All Ryan could think was one thing: *No, that's my man.*

CHAPTER 17

~ *Ryan* ~

The last day of filming was done.

Jordan, Micah, Angie, and the rest were returning to LA, working on that long list of things that Jordan had explained about. The postproduction and sound and footsteps.

There was one last thing to do, stills for marketing. The characters were in costume, standing in various poses, several with the tiny kittens who had made themselves at home with the crew.

Tomorrow was Jordan's last day, and the wrap party would be in his cabin tonight. Of course Ryan was invited. Jordan had texted him and told him to be there if he could, and that they needed to make the most of the night.

Today had been a weird day. An article from Thomas Ivory had appeared on a blog he ran, using the picture of Ryan and Jordan together. But it was a soft article. Nothing about Jordan and Micah's dad, just a pointed exposé on double standards in the B-lists of Hollywood.

Jordan linked Ryan to it in the simple text that read, *I can handle this kind of post*.

There were kisses as well, which made Ryan smile.

And now he was getting ready for his first studio party, and while it wasn't exactly walking down a red carpet with Jordan on his arm for a premiere, it felt pretty damn big.

Ryan stood in front of the mirror, staring at his reflection as though if he looked at it enough, it might change. How would they make long-distance work? How the hell could one of them being in Montana and the other in LA ever be more than a disaster?

He fussed with his hair. The shaggy mess was getting to be more unruly than cute, and he was well overdue a cut. He was in jeans, the ones Jordan said made his ass look a hundred times wonderful. He half turned to see said ass, but it looked quite normal to him. Then he pulled on the dark red sweater that went with his dark brown eyes. That advice came from Ashley this morning, after he'd eaten two pieces of cake in Branches and she'd asked him what was wrong.

He'd said, "Justin's gone, Adam's a mess and keeps calling me, and I don't know what to wear for the wrap party."

Pathetic, really. He was thirty-three, not thirteen.

"Justin will still be gone whether you worry or not," she'd said, topping off his coffee. "Adam is just freaking out because Justin has vanished. And as to what to wear, I love your dark red sweater, the V-neck. It looks lovely with your brown eyes. Now eat the last of your cake and stop fretting."

So here he was: red sweater, check; ass-enhancing jeans, check; hair tidy... sort of. He'd shaved, used aftershave, and was ready. Tonight he wanted to talk to Jordan, find out how they could make this work.

Because he wanted it. Desperately.

He went down to the bar, collected Saul and beer, and together they drove to Crooked Tree.

The wrap party was in full swing. Thirty crew, friends, and staff from Crooked Tree were all in and around the cabin and the tents, which had been attached to the cabin with various ties. There were heaters, tables of food, and drinks, but no sign of Jordan.

"He's in his room," Micah said, after finding him. "He said to go in."

Ryan's stomach twisted. So this was it; this was Jordan saying that he wasn't coming back for the wedding in June, and that actually, while this had been fun, it wasn't going to work long-term. By the time he reached Jordan's door, he'd wavered between sadness and acceptance, and he didn't bother to knock.

"Hey," he said as he closed the door behind him.

God, Jordan looked good. His short hair was styled, and designer stubble was the look he was going for, in an off-white form-fitting shirt over a T-shirt and jeans, and he looked fucking edible.

Jordan said, "I wanted to talk, before…."

"Before what?"

Jordan moved from the window and came to a stop right in front of Ryan. "Before I had beer and you thought I was just making shit up."

"Okay."

Ryan pressed himself against the door which gave him a couple more inches of distance between them. Jordan didn't seem to notice; he turned away from Ryan and began to pace the length of the room. *Step, step, step, turn…* rinse and repeat, all while Ryan's stomach was doing its best to jump into his throat and strangle him. Finally, Jordan stopped.

"On paper it won't work, right? The sheriff in Montana, with all his responsibilities, and the flaky LA B-list actor. You see that, don't you?"

"On paper, yes," Ryan said cautiously. He wasn't going to be the one who said anything out of place and caused the whole house of cards to collapse in on them.

"I've been offered a part in a soap opera—the gay son." He grimaced. "Of course I'm the gay one. Already I'm being stereotyped."

"You've had a lot of offers for gay characters?"

"No, just that one."

"That's not exactly stereotyping, then," Ryan said, and he wished he hadn't when Jordan grimaced again.

"It's the tip of the iceberg. All it takes is one role and then I'm the gay guy in all the shows, and no one will have me in their movies as the straight lead."

"Neil Patrick Harris manages it—"

"Did you miss the bit where I am just a B-list actor?" Jordan said, with heat.

Ryan could see where this was going and his temper spiked. Jordan was sabotaging this from the very beginning.

"Jesus, I should have known, You don't want to even try."

Then he left, because if he stayed, it would be a circle in which they argued and it would end everything anyway. He slammed the door shut behind him and selected the quickest way to the front door, not stopping to talk to anyone.

The cold hit him like a sledgehammer, and it was only then he realized he'd left his coat inside. "Fucking hell," he muttered and headed for the car.

"Ryan! Wait!"

He stopped and turned to see Jordan jogging after him, sliding to a stop three feet away.

"What?" he snapped.

"Don't leave."

"I'm not staying to be pushed into arguing with the man I love over something he has created in his goddamn head. So, no thank you, but I'm leaving until you get your head straight."

He turned away, but Jordan sprinted around him, sliding on the ice and grabbing at Ryan's arm to stop his fall. "Wait, I'm sorry. I love you too."

Ryan wanted to say he'd never told Jordan he loved him, then he realized that was exactly what he'd done. "But it won't work," Ryan finished for him. "Yeah, you said."

"No, I wasn't going to say that." Jordan wrapped his arms around himself. "Please. I want you to say we can work this out."

Ryan ignored the instinct to make him go back inside with his pansy-ass LA cold aversion. "Wait, it's up to me to convince *you*? Is that what you're saying?"

"No, fuck…. No… I fucked this up." He relaxed his arms at his side and shook his hands as if attempting to rid himself of the tension inside him. "We can make it work, right. This is your home, and my home is wherever Micah is. I want to be with you, and I think, with enough patience, we could work around me being in LA for some parts of the year. And if we played things right, I could make a home here with you."

He stepped forward and curled his hands into Ryan's sweater. "I know it's a lot, and you might not even feel like I do—"

Ryan covered Jordan's mouth with a hand to stop him talking. "Yes."

"Yes what?" Jordan asked, his words muffled behind Ryan's hand.

"Whatever we need to do to make this work. That's what."

And then they were kissing, and the cold was the only thing that eventually made them separate.

Hand in hand they went back into the cabin and through the tent, getting a couple of wolf whistles, and Ryan underscored what had happened by bending Jordan back and kissing him with the best kiss of his entire life.

They didn't let go of each other's hands all night.

That was what love was like.

~ *Jordan* ~

Being apart was hard. The hardest. With Skype and texting, they managed to make it to June.

The snow had long since melted and the days were warmer. Ryan had flown out to LA once, hated it. A lot. But he'd tried his best. After all, Jordan was changing his whole life for Ryan, so Ryan felt like he needed to do something back.

They'd rented a house together. That was the first thing that shocked the hell out of Jordan. He and Ryan had actually gone from "I love you" to renting a property together in Montana, a couple of miles from Carter's bar.

Ryan hadn't properly moved in yet; that would be tonight after Eddie and Jenny's wedding.

Jordan was sitting with Adam and Ethan, not quite ready to be a part of the whole brother show that was going on at the front. Anyway, from here he got a very good look at Ryan in his suit, even better when Ryan came over to talk to sit with Jordan, leaning forward when Adam began to speak.

"Ryan, can we talk after?" Adam asked in a soft voice.

Ryan nodded and held Jordan's hand as the music started; Jake and Milly began the bridal procession.

The wedding was beautiful. Eddie grinned from ear to ear and Jenny smiled just as hard, but it was nice to get out of the church and into the early-summer warmth. Weirdly enough, he missed the snow and the utter stillness of the Montana winter. Maybe his LA-ness was slowly fading with each visit back to Montana.

Afterward Jordan, Ryan, Ethan, and Adam moved away from the other guests, and Adam began without any introduction or hedging. "I need you to track down Justin and get him to come home. I want him and Gabe as joint best men at our wedding on Christmas Eve.

Ryan crossed his arms over his chest, tense and stern-looking, and Jordan wished he wasn't standing in the middle of this.

"I have an emergency number," Ryan said with a nod to Ethan.

Adam drew himself tall. "Tell him this. Tell him that if he isn't home by Christmas Eve, then I won't be marrying Ethan."

Jordan glanced at Ethan, who looked utterly destroyed and tense. Was this a joint decision, or did Ethan want something very different?

It seemed that Ryan picked up on the same vibe. "Ethan?" he asked softly.

"I want my brother home," Ethan said immediately. "But he has to know that he and Adam have to talk. There are things Adam needs to know that will give him and Justin some kind of peace. Add that to the text."

"I will."

"What if he doesn't come home?" Jordan asked, because he wasn't sure either Adam or Ethan were really thinking this through with their ultimatum.

Neither of them seemed offended that he asked that. "If he loves us," Ethan began, "either of us, then he'll come home."

"I'll try," Ryan said.

Jordan slipped a hand in the crook of Ryan's arm and leaned on his shoulder, just to be there for support. Ryan relaxed at the touch.

Jordan pulled on Ryan's hand. "Come meet Jenny's family."

That was Ryan's out from the conversation. At that point, Ryan could leave it to Jordan to go alone. After all, Jordan would understand Ryan was in serious mode, but not only did Jordan want to meet this new part of his family, but he wanted to get Ryan away from the intensity of Adam and the fear in Ethan's eyes.

"Are you sure you want him home?" Ryan asked.

Adam paled. "I never wanted him to go," he said, his eyes bright.

"His concern was that he was detrimental to your progress." Ryan sounded like he was quoting from a sheet of notes. Then he added in a softer tone, "But he asks about you when he asks about his dad and Ethan."

"Please tell him, Ryan, tell him I want him to come home, that I know real from nightmares now."

"Do you though?" Ryan asked.

Adam closed his eyes briefly. "Every day I try."

"I doubt I'll be able to change his mind."

"But you'll try?"

"Yes." Ryan moved away, but before they'd taken two steps, he turned back to Ethan and Adam, and nodded at them. "I will do everything in my power to make sure Justin and Sam come home. I promise."

Jordan hoped to hell Ryan could make that happen.

July moved into August, and every time Jordan visited Ryan and then went back to LA, he left a little more of himself back in Montana.

He didn't want to leave Ryan, aware he was building a life in the small town close to Crooked Tree. He knew where to get the best coffee and that Martha had Saturday morning off from the counter at the grocery store to get her hair done, ready for date night. He also knew that she was seventy-three and her boyfriend was a scandalously younger sixty-five. He'd found the best places to park, the perfect sandwich shop, and even gotten an account at the hardware store because he was working on the garden in their rented place.

He wished they weren't renting. The house they were in was a gorgeous two-story colonial-style house, with a large yard and plenty of flower beds to fill with color. He wanted to buy the place.

Every day he was there—hell, every minute—he was at peace, and his script was coming together nicely.

The righteous uproar over his accidental outing had died away. Some other B-list actor was currently front-page news, and when Brad and Angelina split, Jordan was consigned to yesterday's news.

Everyone seemed to have forgotten apart from the channel buying *Snow in Montana*, who'd made some pointed accusations of "planning to deliver a flawed product," whatever the fuck that meant. Something about viewers not being able to "buy into" Jordan's character.

He wrote an email full of explanation, when all he wanted to do was tell them to get lost. But he couldn't alienate them. Darby Films was new, and if it went under, then every penny of their father's estate that had passed to them would be gone.

He didn't care about himself, but Micah, Angie, and the five staff they supported in LA would be destroyed. So, he bit his tongue and played nice, even attended an awards show representing the channel.

No one asked him about his being gay or about Ryan, and he managed to turn the conversation around to the fact that *Snow in Montana* was a romance full of drama. And snow.

That made the interviewer laugh, and Jordan moved on before she could ask any more questions.

When he was next with Ryan, he held him extra close, and Ryan didn't ask why.

Ryan was quiet. He'd contacted Justin, told him that Adam wanted him home. The only reply was from Sam, who said they'd be home. Sam didn't say when, and Justin never spoke about it when he checked in with Ryan.

Seemed that Ryan didn't take making a promise lightly, and he had slipped into worry mode. Adam spent a lot of time talking to Ryan, not about Justin, but about the memories that were slipping into his head at random moments. Not that they made much sense, at least when Jordan was there listening as well. Adam's dreams seemed like things he was making up. Every time, the newest one contradicted the last, and he collapsed again in the middle of September. He was convulsing when Ethan found him.

Ryan called Jordan, to say that Adam was in the hospital undergoing tests, and Ethan was with him.

Jordan wanted to be home. LA was too far away.

Then one day, with Jordan in Montana, the leaves changing color around them and fall promising slower days and colder nights, news reached Ryan and Jordan.

Adam had woken up that morning in hospital, with clear, unequivocal memories of his time in witness protection. Not everything else he'd forgotten, admittedly; there was still nothing about his childhood. He came home, with a possible diagnosis of epilepsy, he was low and needed Ethan all the time.

Just like Jordan wanted and needed Ryan.

Justin and Sam came home in the middle of October, and that was when everything began to change.

CHAPTER 18

~ *Justin* ~

Sam parked the car and reached over to hold Justin's hand. "Ready?"

Sam didn't have to ask if Justin was okay—he was far from okay. They'd been away from here for a long time, and Sam hadn't said he wanted to come home once. But Crooked Tree and Branches were in his blood, as much as the new family he'd begun to make.

They'd spent time with Sam's brother, even stayed with his parents for a while. That hadn't lasted very long, just the one night, because Justin had wanted to grab the nearest object and smash it over Sam's dad's head. The man was a homophobic asshole, and Sam's mom wasn't much better.

Mostly they'd been traveling around the country, and Justin worked through the guilt and the worry. He was afraid that he would never be able to return to Crooked Tree if it was going to hurt Adam. Seeing him triggered Adam's dreams, nightmares, really, and even though Justin hadn't committed those *particular* crimes, he wasn't blameless.

He'd worked for his country, but he'd been lied to. And that was the catalyst of all of this mess.

"Not sure I'll ever be ready," he murmured.

Sam had squeezed his hand for encouragement, and Justin felt reassured. With Sam next to him, he could do anything.

They saw Gabe first. He was leading a family over the bridge to their car, chatting to the kids and grinning. Then he spotted Sam and Justin, and his smile wavered a little. Ever the professional, he waved away the family and then pulled back his shoulders and stalked over to the car.

"You back for good?" he asked as he stopped about five feet away.

Justin's chest tightened when Gabe didn't come any closer. Then he considered that maybe it was him, that he should be moving forward.

"For good," he said and closed the distance to Gabe, stopping right up in his space and waiting. Something in Gabe's eyes, an understanding, maybe, encouraged Justin to tug him close. When Gabe hugged him just as tight, he knew everyone else would be okay.

Apart from, maybe, Adam.

"You're a fucking asshole for leaving," Gabe said into his ear. "But also fucking brave."

"You curse a lot," Justin said.

"Adam's up at the stables. You going to go and see him?"

Justin pulled away from Gabe and nodded. "I'll go straight up there."

"I'll go up to Branches," Sam said.

They'd talked about it in the car, and Justin agreed that he and Adam needed to do this alone, but he had one question. "Should we tell Ethan?"

Gabe shook his head. "Adam's good. He's doing well and hasn't had an episode in a while now. And hell, he'll explain it to you."

Justin zipped up his jacket, crossed the bridge, and took the path to the stables. He owed everyone an explanation—his brother, his dad, his friends, but first of all, Adam.

Stepping inside the stables was coming home, the familiar scents, seeing Easy in his stable with his ears back, looking right at him. Justin couldn't see Adam, and to give himself time to breathe, he fussed Easy and kissed his velvet nose.

"Seems like you always lose me," he murmured against the softness.

"He knows you'll come back, eventually," Adam said from behind him.

Justin swallowed his fear and turned to face his friend, seeing a different man from the one he'd left. Adam looked well, and he didn't have dark circles under his eyes, nor was he carrying the permanent look of exhaustion and wariness. And fuck, he looked good.

"Seems I can't stay away," he murmured.

"You back for real?" Adam asked, his tone even, his hands stuffed in his jacket pockets.

"Yes. Can we talk?"

Adam nodded and turned on his heel to go over to the small office they had in the stables. No more than a stall that had been walled in, it held a table covered in notes and books. Adam didn't take the chair, just leaned against the table there and crossed his feet at the ankles.

Justin pulled the door shut behind them and leaned against it. He had the feeling that Adam was ready to run at the slightest provocation, and he had to be very careful with what he said.

"So I killed people," he began, stopping when Adam winced. Maybe that wasn't the best place to start, but he deserved honesty. "You know that. I didn't kill the men at the ranch or your tattoo artist, and I didn't know you were alive, otherwise I would have found you. Can you accept that from me?"

That was basically what he'd said before he left, but this time the words weren't emotive, but calm and focused.

"I know," Adam said, in that same, eerily focused tone. "I couldn't look at you because you scared me, made me feel uneasy. Like the man I wanted to know and love like a brother wasn't real. I'm done with that now."

"Can we—" Justin stopped himself. He wanted to ask if he and Adam were okay, and had he recalled anything that would make their relationship right again.

"Thank you for going," Adam offered, taking his hands out of his pockets and using them to lean back farther on the desk. "I know it killed you to leave, but I was a mess. My counselor said I was looking for someone to blame, that my brain was playing tricks with me and putting you in situations, creating scenarios. Talking to Ryan helped. He told me some of the facts. I wasn't there when Stretch was shot, so I couldn't have seen it. I was possibly at the ranch when the security guys were killed, but I know it wasn't you I saw there. And, Justin…." He paused and swallowed, as if the emotion was too much for him to contain. He couldn't seem to get the words out.

"What, Adam?"

"I know you didn't leave me back at the bunker. I know everything was out of our control."

"I would never have left you," Justin said. "If I had thought you were alive, if there had been any chance— Hell, Adam, you're my best friend. Thinking you were dead destroyed me."

Adam nodded and then quirked a smile. "Don't tell Gabe that."

Justin reacted to the teasing tone. "Well, of course there's Gabe as well." Then he sobered a little. "Are you still having the dreams?"

"Sometimes, but Ethan being there is a good thing, and they are happening less and less, and not as graphic."

"What have you remembered?"

"Some of the time I was in WITSEC. Nothing before we disappeared—well, nothing concrete, but I did recall the sinking-with-a-rock, G.I. Joe incident."

Justin winced, recalling losing Adam's toy in the lake when they were not more than six or seven. Adam had been gutted, but Gabe, ever the peacemaker, had passed over his G.I. Joe as a replacement. "Not my finest moment, but it did prove rocks sink very well in water."

"A cerebral moment," Adam joked.

Justin held back the tears that choked his throat. "I missed you all, so bad."

"I'm sorry you had to go for me."

"Did you forget the bit about being best friends?"

"Can we hug this out?" Adam asked, his tone unsure.

It was all Justin could do not to rush straight over and lose his cool card.

They embraced and patted backs, and then somehow the hug changed in quality. Less buddies hugging, more intense, Adam gripping him tight and Justin not wanting him to let go.

"Fucking stupid brain," Adam said with emotion.

Justin didn't move, and they didn't separate for the longest time. And when they did, they grinned stupidly.

"Let's go find our men," Adam said.

Justin was more than ready to do that, only as they walked out of the stables, Gabe got to them first. He looked from Justin to Adam and back again, and relief passed over his face.

"I need to talk to you both," he said.

"Is everything okay?" Justin asked, because Gabe looked odd, worried. "We're okay. I'm back to stay."

"That's not it," Gabe said.

Adam stepped forward, concern in his tone. "What's wrong, G?"

"I need to arrange something. Let's go back in." He stalked past them and into the small office, leaning against the desk where Adam had stood earlier. Justin followed and pulled the door closed behind them. "I have something to ask you both," Gabe launched in without introduction and Adam braced himself, ready to run if Gabe wanted to pick at the wound that was just about healing.

"What's up?" Justin asked, cautiously.

Gabe grinned at them. "I'm going to be a daddy," he announced and smacked his hands together. "And I want you two idiots to be adjusted and steady and there for my kid. So, what do you say?"

The question wasn't just about a new addition to the family, it was Gabe making sure everything was okay and that the two of them, Justin and Adam, were good again.

"That's freaking wonderful." Justin pulled Gabe into a hug, and so did Adam, adding his own congratulations.

"When's the baby due?" This was from Adam, who was grinning from ear to ear.

"Would you believe April 1?"

More congratulations and backslapping, guys being guys, friends together, and then they separated. Adam heading off to Ethan, Gabe to his wife, and Justin to mend fences with his dad.

They could make this work, despite this weird dynamic where at any time Adam might recall something that scared him.

Justin could handle it, and it seemed that maybe Adam could as well.

CHAPTER 19

~ *Jordan* ~

Snow in Montana was set to premiere the first Saturday of November, part of a launch of six Christmas movies. The marketing focused on the love story, Montana, the snow, and a kittens, and it was easily the best of those being released.

Or so Ryan told him.

Not that he'd seen the others, or indeed watched the whole of *Snow in Montana*, but Ryan was fiercely loyal and in love with him.

How did I get so lucky?

"Earth to Jordan, come in, Jordan," Ryan said right in his ear, which made him jump and snap out of the sappy feelings he was experiencing.

In answer he rolled farther on top of Ryan and kissed the air out of him. They'd made love and fallen asleep in each other's arms, waking to the peace of a Saturday when Ryan wasn't on duty, and Jordan had nothing more on his agenda than shopping for a tree and then watching the premiere.

Oh, and catering for the hordes who were descending on them.

All four of Ryan's brothers with assorted girlfriends, Jenny, the kids, the Todds and Allenses, and anyone else at Crooked Tree. Everyone was coming for 7:00 p.m., and they needed to open the doors between the dining room and the front room, and move furniture about.

They'd woken to snow, which was fitting, and the cold of a new morning, snuggling back under the covers as Jordan disappeared into his own thoughts.

Finally, Jordan said, "We need to get the tree," as if that was the only thing he'd been thinking about.

"And the rest," Ryan said.

Jordan wanted the house to look festive, with at least a tree ready for the Christmas movie to hit the television, but true to form, the list had grown longer with the week. In the end Ryan had insisted that Sam and Ashley be hired to cater for everyone.

"Okay, I'll tell you what I was really thinking," he murmured against his lover's warm skin. He brushed a kiss over the closest nipple and then across to the other.

"What was that?"

"That I love you."

Ryan chuckled and half rolled so Jordan was under him. "Good thing you do, otherwise I'd feel pretty stupid loving you."

They kissed for the longest time, until his need for the bathroom had Ryan leaving the bed, and Jordan decided it was time to get up. They showered together, which delayed leaving the house due to mutual and very satisfying blow jobs, and it was dark again by the time they set up the tree and hung the decorations that Jordan had bought. The lights were tiny white icicles, and with the main lights low and the tree lit up, the large area looked good.

Sam and Ashley arrived a little after six, and between them they set up the food in the kitchen, with Justin and Gabe arriving together soon after.

Ashley's bump was visible to the point where Jordan had to stop himself from patting her belly and talking to the baby. Josh and Kirsten arrived, plus Ryan's various brothers. Adam and Ethan had driven Marcus and Sophie over, Kirsten brought her boyfriend, and Josh made instant friends with Milly. Luke hovered in the corner, sending baleful looks at Kirsten, and Jordan felt his pain. Unrequited love must be hard.

Nate and Jay were the last to arrive, bringing in a crate of drinks each, some beer, some sodas. Once the door closed on them, everyone who mattered was there. Well, except for Micah and Angie, who'd decided to watch the movie in their hotel room in the Maldives, where they were taking a long-overdue break.

Jordan and Micah had texted that morning, and Micah ending up calling him. He only had one question for Jordan. "Are you happy?"

To which Jordan simply said, "As happy as you are with Angie."

They would be getting together for Christmas, but that didn't mean that Jordan didn't miss his twin. The compromises he had to make to be with Ryan were sometimes hard, but nothing that meant anything was easy, surely?

"Ready?" Ryan wrapped his arms around him from behind and did that whole "leaning his chin on Jordan's shoulder" thing. "Ten minutes."

"What if everyone hates it?" Jordan asked, the only doubt he would allow himself.

Ryan laughed low in his ear. "Not possible," he said. "Now come sit down."

Everyone sat, some on chairs, the two sofas, or cushions on the floor. Ashley had a seat to herself, with Gabe on the floor next to her, his head on her thigh. And then it was seven, and Jordan's work was there for everyone to see.

The movie was smooth, and he watched it from a technical point of view, laughing along with the others over the corny Christmas commercials in the breaks and trying not to be too critical.

"There's Easy!" Justin exclaimed. "He looks so good." Which started a whole debate in the next commercial break over who had the prettiest horse at Crooked Tree. Good-natured teasing and family interaction so sweet it made Jordan want to write it all down to capture it.

"Jesus, how cold was that water?" Gabe asked in the break just after the fight scene.

"So cold you wouldn't believe," Jordan said, shivering at the memory.

"No way would you get me in the river in freaking March," Gabe added.

And so it went, and when the movie ended, everyone clapped and cheered and whistled, and at that moment Jordan felt like the greatest actor on earth.

Not bad for a B-list Christmas romance actor.

Ryan's kiss and hug of congratulations was the icing on the cake.

Likely they'd get sick of the story, scheduled to replay so many times between now and Christmas, but for now it was perfect.

When everyone left, he and Ryan curled up on the sofa under a blanket and watched the movie again.

"Love you," Ryan murmured and pressed a kiss to the top of Jordan's head.

"Love you back," Jordan answered.

Perfect.

Adam and Ethan's wedding took place at Crooked Tree, family and close friends only. It was held in Branches, and a tent took up the space next to Jay's office, for overflow.

The ceremony was beautiful. Jordan held Ryan's hand the entire time that Adam and Ethan exchanged vows.

"I loved you when you were fifteen, and I never stopped loving you," Ethan said. "When I wake in the morning, you are the first person I think about. When I fall asleep, you are the man I hold in my heart. I always knew you would come home to me one day."

Jordan's throat was choked with emotion at the words, and Ryan's grip on his hand was tight.

Adam smiled at Ethan. "I loved you when I was fifteen, I am sure of it—not that I remember." He paused and allowed the group of people around them to smile and laugh at the comment. Then he grew serious. "I know I must have loved you then, because I can't imagine not loving you. When I wake up in the morning, you are the first person I think about, and when I fall asleep in your arms, you are the man I have in my heart. I was always going to come home one day."

The registrar, smiling, pronounced them married, and then they kissed, laughing into the touch and holding each other tight.

Jordan leaned in to Ryan. "One day that could be us." He waited for Ryan to laugh or dismiss the comment—or hell, walk away. "I want it to be us."

Instead, Ryan kissed the end of his nose. "Jordan, I want that too."

LA didn't feel right, like a T-shirt that didn't fit properly or shoes that were too small.

Jordan had only landed that morning, but it had hit him as soon as he stepped out of the terminal. The heat was too much, the people too loud, the light too bright.

Montana was home. Most of all, *Ryan* was home.

Micah collected him from Arrivals.

Stuck in LA traffic, Jordan couldn't keep the feelings hidden away. "I need to move to Montana permanently."

Micah glanced at him. "I know."

"You know?"

"You're my twin, of course I *know*. Darby Films will be fine. We have two projects next year, and you'll star in them both. We can set them in Montana, make romance in Montana our brand. I'll work here, you'll work in Montana, and we'll rack up the frequent-flier miles in visits, yeah?"

Jordan smiled at his brother. "You're sure?"

"Yes."

It really was as easy as that.

Epilogue

~ *Jordan* ~

New Year's Eve. Carter's Bar was filled to capacity. Jordan managed to get through the crowd of dancers and make his way behind the bar. He took two beers and pushed a ten-dollar note into Saul's pocket. Every single time Saul would say it was on the house, but Jordan never felt right about doing that to him.

"He's with Milly and Jake," Saul shouted over the noise of Madonna blaring from the speakers, turning to serve a couple of guys who were literally holding each other up.

Jordan headed out the back, finding the blanket fort exactly where he'd left it that morning. The whole structure had been embellished with even more blankets and more chairs holding up the edges; he pulled back the blanket that formed the door.

He and Ryan were babysitting. Milly, Jake, and Josh were all eating cookies and chatting excitedly.

Ryan lay back on a nest of pillows, smiling up at him. "Come in," he said.

~ *Ryan* ~

Ryan took the proffered beer and scooted over a bit to let Jordan squeeze in next to him.

"So, who are we?" Jordan asked the kids. "Pirates? Cowboys?"

"Children," Josh announced. He was the oldest, and both Milly and Jake looked at him with adoration.

"Just children?" Jordan did his whole cute, fake-pout thing, which Ryan loved.

"*Magic* children," Josh said, as if Jordan was stupid not to have thought of that.

"Are we having an adventure?" Ryan asked, and Jordan elbowed him in appreciation that he was joining in.

The children spun a complicated tale of magic and wizards and dragons, and all Ryan could do was stare at Jordan, wondering how he'd ever got so lucky.

~ *Justin* ~

"How's married life, then, big brother?" Justin asked Ethan, trying to be heard over the music. He handed him a beer.

Carter's was hopping tonight, and with two hours to go until midnight, energy levels were still high.

Ethan took a long swallow of his beer. He looked distinctly uncomfortable with being here. Probably a mix of loud music and the fact that Adam was on the dance floor with Sam. The two of them were in the middle of this hugely complicated dance-off with some other guys, but Ethan was just watching.

"Love it," Ethan shouted, then grinned because he didn't need to say anything else.

Justin tapped his foot to the music, a feeling of peace stealing over him despite the noise and chaos. "I think I'm going to ask Sam to elope," he shouted into Ethan's ear.

Ethan frowned and then thumped him. "No fucking way are you eloping," he announced. His words sounded loud as the music died and segued into the next song.

Quite a few people turned to look at them, Sam included. Sam, who then danced his way over and wound his hands around Justin's neck.

"We're eloping? What if I wanted to wear a white suit and have a big party?" he asked.

Justin held Sam close and didn't ever want to let him go. "Love you," he said.

Sam kissed him, and the kiss didn't end quickly.

This was love, and it was perfect because it put some of Justin's ghosts to rest. And he needed that.

~ *Adam* ~

Ethan tugged Adam out of the main bar and through a door behind it, which opened into a large kitchen area. The muffled thump of music was better than the high-energy noise that made his head rattle. He was done, and really, all he wanted to do was go home with Ethan and celebrate the New Year in private.

Ethan held him tight, kissed him, pressed him back against the wall, and loved him so much that Adam melted against him.

"Hey, Uncle Ethan. What ya doin'? Hi, Uncle Adam."

Ethan backed away. They both looked down at Josh, with his gap-toothed smile, holding a plate of cakes.

"I'm just showing your Uncle Adam how much I love him," Ethan said.

Josh wrinkled his nose and then grinned. "Cool. You wanna come share our fort with us? We're killing dragons, and I'm in charge."

Ethan glanced at Adam with a rueful smile and a question in his eyes.

"We'd love to," Adam said.

Through the door was the noise of public celebration, and he kind of thought it would be good to hide away. A blanket fort seemed like the perfect solution.

Of course, when they crawled in, finding Ryan and Jordan already there, it was a tight squeeze, but it turned out you didn't need much room to kill dragons. And when Justin and Sam joined them, pulling over more chairs to expand the space and stealing the seat cushions from the sofa, Adam couldn't ask for a better way to ring in the New Year.

The kids fell asleep, piled like puppies to one side.

And the grownups? They talked softly about all the dragons they'd battled the last few years.

And the New Year was filled with hope.

THE END

HAVE YOU READ?

If you enjoyed Montana, you may like the Texas Series. Charting the love of Jack and Riley Campbell-Hayes, from marriage by blackmail, through murder, intrigue, and above all family, the Texas series is complete in seven novels.

The Heart of Texas

Riley Hayes, the playboy of the Hayes family, is a young man who seems to have it all: money, a career he loves, and his pick of beautiful women. His father, CEO of HayesOil, passes control of the corporation to his two sons; but a stipulation is attached to Riley's portion. Concerned about Riley's lack of maturity, his father requires that Riley 'marry and stay married for one year to someone he loves'.

Angered by the requirement, Riley seeks a means of father's stipulation. Blackmailing Jack Campbell into marrying him "for love" suits Riley's purpose. There is no mention in his father's documents that the marriage had to be with a woman and Jack Campbell is the son of Riley Senior's arch rival. Win win.

Riley marries Jack and abruptly his entire world is turned inside out. Riley hadn't counted on the fact that Jack Campbell, quiet and unassuming rancher, is a force of nature in his own right.

This is a story of murder, deceit, the struggle for power, lust and love, the sprawling life of a rancher and the whirlwind existence of a playboy. But under and through it all, as Riley learns over the months, this is a tale about family and everything that that word means.

www.rjscott.co.uk

RJ Scott

RJ's goal is to write stories with a heart of romance, a troubled road to reach happiness, and most importantly, that hint of a happily ever after.

RJ Scott is the bestselling gay romance author of over ninety MM romance books. She writes emotional stories of complicated characters, cowboys, millionaire, princes, and the men who get mixed up in their lives. RJ is known for writing books that always end with a happy ever after. She lives just outside London and spends every waking minute she isn't with family either reading or writing.

RJ also writes MF romance under the name Rozenn Scott.

The last time she had a week's break from writing she didn't like it one little bit, and she has yet to meet a bottle of wine she couldn't defeat.

She is always thrilled to hear from readers, bloggers and other writers. Please contact via the following links below:

Email: rj@rjscott.co.uk
Webpage: www.rjscott.co.uk
Facebook: https://www.facebook.com/author.rjscott
Twitter: https://twitter.com/rjscott_author